NECKLACE / CHOKER

THE SLOVAK LIST

Jana Bodnárová

NECKLACE / CHOKER

then, meanwhile, now.
/a small novel in fragments/

TRANSLATED BY

JONATHAN GRESTY

LONDON NEW YORK CALCUTTA

SERIES EDITOR: *Julia Sherwood*

This book has received a subsidy from SLOLIA Committee,
the Centre for Information on Literature in Bratislava, Slovakia

Seagull Books, 2021

First published in Slovak as *Náhrdelník/Obojok* by Jana Bodnárová
© Jana Bodnárová, 2016

First published in English by Seagull Books, 2021
English translation © Jonathan Gresty, 2021

ISBN   978 0 8574 2 890 5

British Library Cataloguing-in-Publication Data
A catalogue record for this book is available from the British Library.

Typeset by Seagull Books, Calcutta, India
Printed and bound by Versa Press, East Peoria, Illinois, USA

This book may never have come about without the life and work of the painter, Ernest Špitz. He was its prime inspiration, though his own life can be seen here only intermittently.

*

/To Janko, Baška and Juraj/

Now/fragment/

MIDDLE OF THE NIGHT, AN ABANDONED HOUSE,
A FORGOTTEN GARDEN.

Sára.

A sultry night, phantom voices, eddies of wind . . . The house cracking, creaking, whistling: its wood, glass, furniture, wallpaper, floorboards. And then, when Sára turned on the lights, the bodies of moths crackled with a deathly sound on the bare lightbulbs.

How many people pass through life, undiscovered, like those moths, or like summer annuals, fleeting, weightless, almost invisible, ashamed they even exist for no one will miss them, removing almost all trace of themselves after their gossamer-like existences? With such thoughts, Sára sat down on the bed.

If an occasional car passed along the street at night, perhaps a taxi with a passenger for the night train bound for the nearby station, shadows shimmered across the walls. Like translucent belly dancers, they slipped across the once-green wallpaper with silver shells, then disappeared.

The sounds of the house awakened Sára; at night, they revived and were released from their silent captivity. Surely it was those sounds that roused her from her sleep, not the trains or the cars. She was used to those from her flat. The voices of the villa roused

3

but didn't trouble her, though. They were intimate, confidential and hers alone. She felt the dust and the mustiness in her nostrils—she had not had time during the day to properly clean out this, her old bedroom.

After the scorching day, the night was cool, damp and pleasant and enticed Sára out into the garden. It was just as wild and abandoned as the house, only its sounds were different. The wind fluttered the leaves, making them rustle for a moment. For Sára, it was another familiar sound—like that of an arrow when fired from a bow. She picked out the shape of the abandoned flower bed. Tulips, crocuses, pansies, dahlias, petunias, slipper orchids, hortensias and autumn asters used to grow there, and all had left confused signals and traces behind them.

Everything was listening to the night-time silence, even the silence itself.

Sára gazed into the depths of the garden and it seemed that at the far end a vagrant girl was sleeping, a drug addict perhaps. But when she drew closer, through the long grass, she saw only a clump of thistles and dock leaves. And then, unexpectedly, she scratched her forearm on a wild rosebush. She shuddered and squealed slightly; a bird, roused from its sleep, twittered, and a cat hissed, perhaps one with its shelter in the garden or one that had lost its shyness and fear and was gravitating towards sleeping humankind. Sára breathed a sigh of relief. It wasn't a girl lying in the garden, after all! Of course there are neglected children who wander the streets and sleep in deserted gardens, unseen like those moths in the house a moment before. And such deserted gardens attract people. They are like hotels—places for temporary journeys, overnights, discoveries, losing oneself, sex, murders, suicides . . .

She sat on the rickety old bench and looked at the dilapidated summerhouse, or 'garden parlour', as Sára's mother used to call it. Sára would be so happy to see her mother again: drying her hair after washing it with egg shampoo, tilting her head so that her long blonde mane could almost touch the ground, running her fingers through it and listening to a song on the radio coming through the open window:

'Turn off the lanterns, I want to see the dark. He hasn't come, he hasn't come . . . let the fireflies lead me home . . .'

Mama sang in the summer house together with the high-pitched female voice on the radio. There was a smell of pea soup and freshly cut parsley, mixed in with the scent of lilac and exhaust fumes from the road.

Sára would like to sit like that for a long time on the old bench. Someone had stolen its snake-shaped metal armrests and one of the wooden planks forming the backrest was also missing but she could still sit there for hours in the swirling breeze of the summer night. The moon was like a burnished crystal bowl, greenish in colour. A black-green beetle was making its way up the leg of her pyjamas, and it occurred to her how much life, miniature and alert, there was in an abandoned garden. It was not a dead place at all. She had woken up just one of those tiny sleeping creatures!

She would breathe in those opiate fragrances and think of nothing in the abandoned garden. She used to scatter all her toys among those flowers and bushes, coddling, threatening and even shouting at them. She was not afraid of frogs or lizards on rocks, nor of mice emerging from their hideaways in late autumn. She would catch them by their tails, and, when they started screeching and swinging from side to side, would let them go. She remembered how a man, probably her father, lifted her up high and she was afraid he would drop her and break her bones. It would be like when she threw a stone at her chubby little doll which always rolled over onto its belly and for a moment would go on rocking comically. Sára wanted to know the reason why it rocked like that but could only do so by smashing open the round belly of the green doll with its wide eyes and cheeks and lips painted a bright pink.

A curtain patterned with birds fluttered out from an open window. Sára hadn't closed the door behind her and there must be a draught because something was banging inside, perhaps the door she had left open. But she had no reason to be alarmed: there was no girl sleeping there, no cheap prostitute from the railway station used to men's hands rather than the spiders and other insects that would now be exploring her. No dock leaves, the fans of geishas, would be fanning her. A thin cloud filtered out the brightness of the moon; Sára imagined it had, at that moment, the same colour as a lake she could see to the bottom of, a place deep down where things went on which no one had yet discovered. She had come back to that place, her father and grandparents' house after many years, like a diver going down to the very bottom of that lake to discover submerged things hidden among the algae, soft and indistinct.

It was after nine when Sára woke up. She felt refreshed despite her interrupted sleep and climbed out of her sleeping bag. She found a metal mug in the old sideboard and put some water on the stove to boil so she could make herself some Turkish coffee. At the top of the sideboard were a few earthenware plates, bowls and cups left there by the last tenants. Deep in its recesses lingered the scents of cinnamon, cloves, vanilla and spices, all of which her mother and grandmother must have once kept in its small wooden drawers. The familiar scents had remained there for decades and Sára breathed them in deeply. She then filled a bowl with some cereal she had bought the day before and poured some yogurt on top. She sipped her honey-sweetened coffee and made a shopping list on a scrap of paper: detergent, bread, butter, milk, tea, sardines, vegetables, fruit . . .

Sára went shopping on an old bicycle she had found the day before in the conservatory. It had once been a magical part of the villa, metal framed, with the lengths of steel on its walls and low cupola creating secessionist curves. Large areas were glazed and inside, like in an enormous upturned galley, sailed the exotic pilgrims of the botanical world. Of the plants that had once grown there, there were still stubborn tufts of grass growing as well as ivy reaching up to the ceiling in search of light and the rainwater that leaked through cracks in the glass. A few wicker armchairs were scattered around, two old chests of drawers, watering cans, flowerpots with dried plants like the skeletons of reptiles. One of the later tenants had painted some of the conservatory glass a milky-white colour— now it was as if the room had been blindfolded. The day before, Sára had pumped up the tyres on the bike, dusted off all its cobwebs and unjammed the screeching brakes. She had found a can of oil, and was soon able to cycle off to the shops.

She went first to the chemist's and grocer's and then to the outdoor market to buy fruit and vegetables. And then, just as she was putting some summer squash and a sack of potatoes into the basket at the back of the bicycle, a woman grabbed her by the shoulder. She had pinkish eyes, white hair, eyebrows and eyelashes, and seemed to be convulsing as saliva oozed from the corner of her mouth. The woman then dropped her shoulders and hung like a ragdoll around Sára's neck. Sára screamed but a second later remembered herself, and, with the help of one of the stallholders, sat the albino down on an upturned crate next to the counter. The epileptic fit did not last long before that peculiar woman, bleached of all colour, stood up, dusted off her dress, straightened her hair, wiped her face with a handkerchief and left without a word.

The poor woman's lucky she wasn't born in Africa! shouted out the Bulgarian seller from the vegetable stall opposite. Sára had wanted to buy an aubergine and sweet Canadian onion from him.

Her only chance of survival (he continued) would be in a camp where albinos are kept hidden from their murderers. When they catch such a girl, they chop off her arms and legs to sell—and they get twice as much for her head . . . They find some madman who does black magic with the body parts to make sure the highest bidder wins the elections.

Sára had also read something barbarous about how, in Tanzania, such people without pigment were considered to be spirits with eternal life, that panaceas for various illnesses were made from their limbs and that fishermen wove their luminous hair into their nets because it would help them catch more fish.

Sára recalled how many years before she had seen an albino sparrow, all white, in the local natural history museum. It was on display somewhere away from all the other normally coloured birds.

There will always be white sparrows everywhere, she thought! Excluded and disowned, on the edge of society.

Don't worry, madam. We're used to her here. She's always around, looking at everything but not buying very much. It happens to her quite often.

So said the market seller cheerfully as she went on weighing tomatoes. But Sára stood dumbstruck, shaken by the scene and what the Bulgarian had said.

Later she bought a cup of coffee from a man with a coffee maker on a tricycle and a bunch of strong-smelling carnations from the nearest florist's. Leaning against the bike, she was able to unwind as she watched people coming and going and listened to the stallholders and customers haggling over prices around those richly coloured carpets of flowers and vegetables. Sometimes a little gipsy child ran up to her begging for money; in the pocket of her canvas bag she had some coins she could give them. The children then ran back to their mothers who were selling from buckets the first blueberries and mushrooms from the nearby mountains. The sound of the bell from the Gothic church momentarily interrupted the hubbub.

Sára went straight home from the market. She had to take down the net curtains in her old bedroom and wash them, clean the windows and the floor once more, dust the furniture and scrub the kitchen so that she could bear living there for a while. She didn't know for how long she would have to wait for the first potential buyers to come. Or perhaps her meeting with the mayor would decide everything.

Again she wandered through the empty rooms on the ground-floor before ascending the oak staircase, once so painstakingly polished, up to the first floor. She passed through the bedrooms where there were shadows on the walls in places where pictures had hung or heavy pieces of furniture had once stood. She recalled where there had once been chests of drawers, armchairs, ottomans, a bookcase, a piano and a Venetian mirror inherited from her father's parents. A few sticks of furniture remained, but all the inlaid pieces had long gone. The tenants must have sold them to an antiques dealer. Who knew what had happened to the piano upon which Sára's mother used to keep a little carpet and Hanukkah menorah as a memento of the mother-in-law she never knew. A metal spiral staircase took Sára up into the attic.

Sára's earliest memories were from within the walls of the villa, hanging intangibly in its space, shimmering in its air.

Before the fate of the villa was to be decided, however, a meeting with Iboja awaited Sára. When in the early evening, she stretched out contentedly on the freshly cleaned floor, she observed the dancing shadows on the ceiling, changing with the movement of the sun, and recalled the strange dream which Iboja had written to her about.

Now/fragment/

TWO SWANS.

EACH ONE FLYING IN THEIR OWN SILENCE.

Iboja, the house.

My little sister,

What a joy that you are coming, both because of what I wrote to you last and because of everything that has (and hasn't) happened between and around us! Between us two black swans—each of us flying in our own silence. We will be together again in the house where you once lived—as I'm sure you remember! Your villa was near our Hotel Aurora—which no longer exists—at least not in the true sense of the word (there's a lot here you won't recognize). The building's so different! You'll still see the statue of Aurora, torch in hand, on the cupola. But the sign has gone. The Communists added a diacritic to the O but now it's all gone, you can just make out the negative in the plaster but who would notice it?! The houses of our friends and relatives have disappeared; their Christian cemetery went ages ago as has our Jewish one. Only the churches have remained untouched, and the synagogue has finally been restored— they now hold concerts and exhibitions there. There are huge shops here now, like you have in the West. In fact, that's where they have come from. In the buildings and yards on the square and main street you won't find any of the little old shops you knew. All you'll find are clothes shops with big brash signs saying: 'English Second-Hand'. Or Asian shops stacked high with cheap clothing, shoes and sports goods. And in the old tailors', ironmongers', drapers' and tobacconists' premises, you'll just find endless pizzerias and coffee shops. Even I no longer know now what those shops all used to be. There is a cakeshop in the place where that milkbar was for many years—that place you always found so smelly! Only the bank has stayed in the same place with bars on its windows and grandiose columns. But it no longer belongs to a 'historically changeable' country like ours but to someone from outside. In fact, no one here really knows who it belongs to.

You're my little sister and will always remain so even though we have both grown old! Time is a draught and the years blow past. And you can't keep illnesses away.

I'm glad we'll have the chance to sort out your villa. As you know the last tenants moved out three years ago and since then it's been going to ruin. I'm glad you don't want to leave it to its fate, though. Tramps sometimes sleep in the garden and perhaps some of them even go inside, though I check the locks and none seem to have been broken. The town wanted to make it a museum for your father but some of the councillors were against it. I've been bothering the town hall for years because of it! But you know how it is—everyone has their own vested interests. Some would like to have the place demolished and then be bribed into giving planning permission for an apartment block. It's a big plot of land. Or some firms might want to have a fitness centre there, perhaps. It's important to always be young and beautiful, even in our little town!

I'm glad you're coming and will decide when you're here what to do with the place. I actually dreamt about it not long ago. At first in my dream I could see only a huge sea with lots of human bodies bobbing on the waves—all lifeless, like rubber dolls. And then everything started gushing into the rooms of your house. They were empty, but the floors were flooded with muddy, stagnant water. I could still hear footsteps on them, though—and echoes of footsteps. What a nightmare! Almost nothing happened in it but my heart was still pounding when I woke up!

And I'll be glad to see you again after all these years. Time slips by so fast!

With hugs,

Iboja

Now/fragment/

A DARK NIGHT IN THE GARDEN.

Iboja and Sára.

The evening warmth stole through the garden. On the table stood a candle in a Chinese lamp, a bottle of red wine, glasses; there were savoury scones in little baskets and plates of sliced cheese, olives, hazelnuts and almonds. Sára had carried the table down from the attic the day before, then washed it with soapy water and a brush. She found an old damask tablecloth in the chest of drawers; it had a few rust stains on it but she still laid it on the table. The scent of the remnants of flowers, the grass and the leaves on the trees was getting stronger.

You've done wonders in such a short time! It's like a home again. Almost like in the old days, said Iboja.

Like when Mama used to listen to 'Turn off the lanterns / I want to see the dark / He hasn't come, he hasn't come . . .' sang Sára.

They both laughed and then after a moment started to sing the old song together:

Millions of fireflies
Light my way home
The moon is not shining
And my sweetheart hasn't come . . .

Your father loved Emilka very much, began Iboja.

And she him! She never married again. She once had an admirer . . . oh yes . . . but I huffed and puffed and said: Get him away from us! And just imagine—she listened to me! Children can be really cruel . . . Sára sipped from her wine as she spoke.

There was no one like your father. Emilka would have got rid of any other man whoever he was. The sooner, the better!

Shadows flashed across Sára's face. For a moment she couldn't speak and then she said:

Today I was rummaging through the attic in the hope I might find something else Dad had left. An old canvas no one had noticed; a few drawings . . . A sketchbook, perhaps . . . And I found something. Look at this sketch. Who could it be?

Sára flattened out the yellowed paper with her hands:

It is not a child—the proportions are all wrong. See how it seems to be playing a flute in some kind of an abstract place. And what's all the vegetation? Aren't they the leaves of a tree?

Putting the little sketch as close to the light as they could, the two women examined it together.

Sára! It'll be Eliška Beňadiková! She taught your father to play the flute. That must be her standing in front of the window. She was the only person in town with curtains crocheted with orange-tree leaves! Auntie Zuzka made them for her.

Iboja gulped down her wine and Sára immediately poured her another glass. For a moment both looked at the dark colour of the wine as the surface rippled.

Eliška and her husband had died long ago, and the old tenement building they moved into from their family townhouse had been demolished.

Iboja could barely remember the old house they had been moved out of after the war to go into a tenement block for labourers from the leather works. The workshops, with their stink of soaking cattle hide, had stretched out at the back of their new home.

Iboja went on:

The workshops and old factories have all gone. In the 1950s, the state insisted on tenants moving into the villa because it was allegedly too big for just your father and grandfather. But later, after Imro died and the block was demolished, your mother let the Beňadiks live out their lives here. All kinds of people once lived here.

Mama and I moved to my grandparents' flat. It was a few years after my father's death. It was easier for Mama to look after me there.

Your mother helped other people, too, while she could, renting out the villa for peanuts! She wanted to keep the house because of you. But later everything changed.

I found something else I want to show you, Iboja—a shellac record. And, though you won't believe it, I found a gramophone too! You'll be as amazed as I was when you see it.

Sára laughed and ran to the house. A moment later she opened one of the high casement windows in the conservatory and the dramatic and scratchy sounds of an alto singing to a tango rhythm came out from the darkness of the house. It was a Polish song and it was called 'One Dark Night'.

'Ciemna dziś noc,
Świszczą kule po stepie i znów
Za depeszą depeszę przez mrok
Wiatr po drutach przesyła.

Wiem, że tę noc
Znowu spędzisz do świtu bez snu ...'

Sára brought the record cover outside with her. On it was a woman's face with even features, dark eyes, high-arched eyebrows and hair pinned back. Below, written in bold, the name—WIERA GRAN.

Iboja suddenly remembered another night, another scene. For a moment the vision of it eluded her; then it returned. Behind her lowered eyelids she saw it as mistily as if it was happening behind shattered glass. She saw an old couple. A similar sentimental song was playing . . . Iboja's grandparents, resting against each other, moving slowly in what was almost an imitation of dancing. Tears were flowing from their eyes. Everything was starting to turn harsh and uncertain for them.

With exaggerated delight in her voice, Iboja said:

Dear Sister! This is like in paradise. Wine, nibbles, a lantern, moonlight—only one thing missing and that's dancing! So let's go and sway on the patio, where I used to push you in your pram like my own sister—together with your cat. Once you sucked her tail and I think you also bit her because she scratched you! For the first time ever, Emilka was really furious with me! She didn't let me push your pram again for ages afterwards.

OK. May I?

Sára got up first.

OK, Sister.

The two women started to dance on the flagstones of the path between which moss, grass and the leaves of long blown dandelions were breaking through. Was it a tango they were dancing? Beneath the dance and their tipsy woman's laughter was the isolation, loneliness and fragility of them both. And then a voice both hoarse and velvety entered the mix:

'*Ciemna dziś noc,*
Step rozdziela nas czarny i zły,
I dlatego nie słyszysz mych słów,
Gdy wiatr świszcze i kule.'

Perhaps the record was scratched or the needle was blunt but in places the voice crackled and jumped. It was the same with the musical instruments—as if they were afflicted with some illness. Both women had the feeling they had entered the past: the music had taken them into another zone where similar songs were sung. And all that was bad and painful about that past was temporarily forgotten.

The two women were now lying in the big bed in Sára's old room and couldn't stop laughing what with all the wine they had drunk and the memories. Then, tucked into their sleeping bags, they again sang the chorus of the song on the record by the Polish singer with the sad eyes, arched eyebrows and sharp features. That record, the only one of many, had for some mysterious reason appeared up in the attic like a secret cipher:

'*Ciemna dziś noc . . .*'

Why had Father put away that one record so carefully?

Sára clearly remembered how the shellac records had for years gathered dust in the space below the stairs down to the cellars—stored in an old cupboard that nobody opened. Before she had even started going to school, while she was still exploring the house—

its recesses and cupboards with an infant's excitement, Sára had come across the black records with their paper sleeves and distinctive smell.

He had lost interest in all the others. For some reason he had hidden just the one.

Perhaps Imro thought you would one day listen to it together. Or perhaps he had some other reason which we will never know.

Sára murmured her agreement and then asked slyly:

Tell me more about what my father was like! A few photos and self-portraits have remained . . . it's true. But he is so dark in them all! Almost tragic! But surely he must have sometimes been fun. Didn't women find him sexy? I bet they flirted with him and tried to seduce him—at least before my mother came on the scene. Tell me! I want to hear it again!

Sára sat up sharply and Iboja turned onto her side to face her.

I was expecting that! I thought you'd ask what he was like again.

And then, with Sára listening eagerly, she told her how Imro was like a magnet to women. Tall, lean, with a pale face and a gleam in his dark eyes—as if he had come from the worldly and remote West. Next to him, the local men with their dialects and sing-song accents were clumsy and charmless. With dark, slightly wavy hair, combed back, receding from an early age, he would always wear a black corduroy suit when he went out—like a uniform making him different from everyone else. Iboja never heard him shout; he spoke softly and said little. There was a sadness that emanated from him . . . Perhaps it was his air of mystery that women found attractive. They thought that their devotion could dispel his sadness. And that he would want to paint them lying on a divan, would canoodle with them and then make love to them. They would be his obsessive lovers—his muses! But he had other bigger plans! He wanted to create a theatre of light in which he would combine music, movement, light and visual art—all together, equally. He kept sending letters to all the offices . . . And he did have some success. They gave him money for a tape recorder, stage lights and speakers . . .

He was the star of his own little theatre—you have the photos of him made up like a clown . . . But a few years later he was taking strong medication and put on a lot of weight. And then he lost it all . . . You know it from the photos . . .

Iboja, struck by the intensity of her memories, then described how he had to abandon his plans of a new experimental theatre even though he struggled in his quest like an Old Testament prophet. And then he painted such a prophet towards the end when all he did was paint and Emilka sometimes had to tie the brush to his hand so that it wouldn't slip from his fingers.

He once showed me the garden, ours I mean . . . Next to the Hotel Aurora . . . I was five and he had started studying painting in Prague . . . He held me in his arms in the living room and we looked out at the garden through the window. It was winter—the time of Hanukkah. He talked about how the evening snow had a special white colour. And about blue-darkness and some force which in the evening scatters diamonds. And that I should never be afraid—of anything or anybody!

Iboja also spoke of how when he came for the holidays, Imro always went to the hotel to see her grandfather—Štern. He treated Imro like his son because he, Štern, was friends with Sára's grandfather. In those times, he helped everybody as much as possible.

He was also very fond of your grandmother. 'Irmuška, my dark beautiful one—the cleverest woman in town,' he would say to her. But you didn't know her.

Sára shook her head. She was lying serenely on her back again:

Strange! I also remember him holding me in his arms. It was in our garden for a change. He lifted me up high. It was certainly him! It must have been! It is about all I can remember of him. I was terrified he would drop me . . . I think I was only three then, or even younger?!

Tears trickled from the corner of Sára's eye down her cheek and into her ear.

It must have been him. He died when you were three-and-a-half.

Iboja was thinking how some memories exhaust the mind and then disappear like groundwater. And then they come up again and create a sudden flood. But you can't always rely on your memory and shouldn't let it reduce you to a bundle of sadness!

I remember it but it's as if the whole scene happened under water. Father playing the violin and Mummy holding me in her arms. He singing along while Mama danced with me across the room and also sang . . . '*Tum-bala, tum-bala, tum-balalaika . . .*'

And then the two of them, all at once burst into song:

'*Tum-bala, tum-bala, tum-balalaika.*
Tum-balalaika shpil balalaika
Tum-balalaika freylik zol zayn.'

When they stopped singing, Iboja turned over to lie on her back again and Sára went back to what she had found in the attic:

Why do you think he left that canvas? It must have had some special meaning for him. The drawing was wrapped up with a little parcel tied up with string. I only noticed it by chance, hidden behind one of the rafters.

Iboja said to the ceiling:

Our closest people have all gone, Sárinka! All emigrated from existence and left us here alone, dear sister! Of course, you still have a few close relatives, with some youngsters among them. But I don't understand them at all. They're such a changeable, adaptable generation—turning to face all sides. We were just little, private anarchists, held back by this small town. But we knew how to rebel, we really did! Though more on the inside than the outside. And perhaps we've remained rebellious inside, haven't we?!

They both chuckled for a moment and then Sára said:

You still have a mother, though.

Oh, Mama! If you want, Sára, we can go and see her. But we can't ask her anything—not even if we wanted to!

How old is she now?

Twenty-five years older than me.

Ninety-five?

Exactly.

Forty years older than me.

You are still young compared to us!

Mademoiselle, your grandchildren are crying!

And liberated by the wine, they both giggled; through the open window came the sounds of a train rumbling in the distance and an occasional car going past, sounds as reassuring as an old lullaby.

But Iboja then said something which unsettled Sára:

And what exactly happened to your grandmother, Imro's mother, during the war? No one ever talked openly about it. It was a taboo subject.

It really was!

Sára had a photograph of her grandmother on her wall at home and knew all the details of her face. She was pale, slightly fleshy of face, with big eyes that looked out piercingly. She had an aquiline nose, jutting chin and hair vigorously tied into a bun . . .

Iboja, I never believed it was suicide! She even wanted to set up a nursing school here. I think she was just suffocating in that cellar and desperately needed some fresh air. Despite everything. She just wanted to walk through the woods and settle her nerves. And something . . . a stray bullet . . . a fragment of something . . . must have hit her.

I also think that's what happened!

Iboja took her hand from the sleeping bag to stroke Sára's face.

And your father was still a child—a boy at a sensitive age. And I think the illness he later had was a result of what he had to go through in that cellar under the forest.

I can barely remember my mother and her parents. It's not enough to give me much sense of my family roots, is it? asked Sára.

That's why we're like sisters! I was also cast out from the warm family nest! But the two of us are wild women! Women who used to run with wolves. Though now I'm just an old mangy she-wolf. A daughter of a she-wolf. Only my sharp teeth have remained!

Iboja laughed so much she started coughing. And then Sára started talking about the book she was reading. Books were her endless source of energy.

Soon their voices started to falter and their breathing slowed and became softer. Sára could see the face of the albino and something like a sparrow's body attached to it. Iboja could hear the howling of wolves in the snowy mountains. The soothing white turned dark grey and the two women fell asleep almost simultaneously.

Now/fragment/

WAITING FOR THE SEA.

Woman—shell.

Sára and Iboja decided before lunch to go to the pension. They had to walk along the railway line for a while before they reached the foot of the hill. The sun still wasn't high up in the sky so they walked quickly. They had to go up a travertine flight of steps to get to the top of the hill alongside which was a military cemetery with a huge bronze statue of some soldiers at its entrance.

It's rather strange. Didn't there use to be a lot more graves here?

Sára could hardly recognize the place. She seemed to remember a huge pattern of little graves and bronze plaques on each of them.

Now the area was much smaller with strictly demarcated spaces for graves and inconspicuous little signs on them, grassy borders on either side of the steps and wildflowers growing from them. In the distance, an old woman was bent down in the grass, picking herbs and mushrooms and putting them in her bag. Nearby a little boy was playing and singing war songs of his own invention in his deepest voice:

'Left, right, left, right. The soldiers are going to fight, to fight. Left, right, left, right . . . !'

Iboja stopped to take a breath, drank from her bottle of water and said:

Apparently the bones of the Russian soldiers have all been removed and taken somewhere. Only the Ruthenian soldiers and ours are still here . . . Here and there you may also find some Hungarian and French names . . . I hope those Soviets weren't killed right here. Now there's just grass and wildflowers growing here—and daisies in spring! But it's quite nice vegetation to have on one's grave, isn't it?

Iboja raised one finger up into the air and laughed ironically.

I made my pioneer vows by the memorial. You, too, Iboja?

You did, but I wasn't allowed. I was of the wrong stock with Grandfather a bourgeois parasite as well as a Jew. And I had parents who had fled to the West. Haha! We thought it would go on for ever!

Iboja waved her hand and cleared her throat as if trying to cough up a memory from her ailing lungs worn out by heavy smoking and the long walk.

At the summit of the hill stood a travertine pylon with a bronze star at the top. Around were travertine benches and withered wreaths leaning against the reliefs of soldiers. Sára took baguettes and bottles of mineral water from her knapsack. Decades before, they would go there with their botany teacher to collect wildflowers. Children would gleefully go and sit in the huge bronze basins of the memorial where every year eternal flames would be lit to mark the anniversary of the end of the war. The metal would glisten in the sun.

But now the bronze was a grey-black and Sára was struck by how shabby and uncared for it was. She could still recall the white gleam of the stone and the gold of the metal when she came here as a grammar school student with her boyfriend—a student in the next class. They would come to smoke cigarettes, kiss, and, especially in the July heat, to caress each other's bodies. Under the low-lying branches of the spruces, they made their first discoveries and she had her first experience of conjugal sex with that lovesick boy whose name she could no longer remember. Not alone like before, when in a fit of desire she would lie in bed at home and squeeze her little breasts before moving her hand down over her belly, thrusting her groin upwards and touching herself as she sighed audibly.

It was easier for them both going downhill but they missed the open space and the mountain ridges in the distance. Now they walked down through the dry deadness of a spruce and pine forest so thick the light darkened into a green-grey and the air also cooled like a cadaver.

When they came out of the wood, they followed a narrow path down the hill through a stretch of fragrant meadow. Ahead of them they could see the pension and a garden with a high fence; beyond it, a stream glistened in the sunlight, and in the distance they could see housing blocks on a huge estate. A man with a watering can and unnaturally jerky movements was watering a little patch of weedy ground marked out with pegs.

He's a retired teacher and thinks he has a garden here in which he grows exotic flowers, Iboja explained to the startled Sára, who stood watching him for a moment.

But the man with the jerky, hurried movements did not notice the two women. He was too busy cursing the hooligans who had again snapped his strings during the night.

He brings water down from the stream and is swearing because he keeps tying up the hanging branches of the wild bushes. In his mind they're the same decorative trees he once had as a biology teacher in his garden at home. It is the wind that snaps the string but he thinks it's some layabouts who do it and so he keeps tying them up again. The staff let him get on with it. So long as it keeps him occupied!

In front of the pension, on benches in the shade of the fenced garden, the residents were sitting like old marionettes. The women and men wore the same straw hats and they all sat staring silently ahead of them. They did not notice the two visitors. Iboja spotted her mother behind a trolley with a jug of water and plastic cups on it. She was sitting motionlessly, the same hat on her head and a handbag held tightly at her side. Iboja kissed her on the cheek, pressed her mother's hand to her forehead and cheeks but the old woman didn't stir.

Mami, it's me, Iboja. And look who I've brought. Imriško's daughter Sára . . .

Sára stroked the old woman's emaciated shoulder and took some chocolate from her bag. She pressed it into the woman's motionless hand, as thin and lifeless as a leather glove. Her face, shaded by her hat, remained hidden.

Do you want some chocolate? This is from Sára.

Iboja's mother didn't react but when Iboja wanted to take the handbag from under her elbow, she bristled and pulled it away.

When I come, I always find two things in her handbag: dried-up lipstick and stale bread . . . Mami, I'll give the bread to the pigeons and the crows . . . Iboja is allowed to. . . . You'll let Iboja do it.

I-bo-ja.

The invalid spoke slowly but clearly. She then relaxed her arm and Iboja took from her handbag some slices of dried bread and put them down next to the bench. Then with Sára she sat down alongside her mother.

Doesn't she speak anymore? asked Sára, disconcerted by the sight of this thin shell of a human body seemingly drained of everything from within. It was as if the old woman's brain, deprived of reason, was merely floating in a skull almost stripped of all hair.

She sometimes says some words in French. From time to time, the carers think she is swearing at them. And I bet she really lets them have it! She's spent almost her whole life in Paris and gets angry when they put the furniture back after she moves it. You wouldn't believe how determined she is to move it . . . She moves her locker and chair and sometimes puts her armchair out in the corridor. Where does she get the strength from?! No one can believe it.

Iboja's expression had turned sad.

Years ago I brought her back here from abroad. It's close so I can often come to see her even if she doesn't recognize me. Without my help she never calls me by name, though. She has even forgotten her own. We're like shadows to her—or echoes. Sounds and shades. I think that's how she perceives us.

The sisters filled the cups with water and carried them along the bench on a tray. Occasionally, the young intern there had to hold a mug to someone's lips and coax them into drinking. When the sun went down, the old men and women would go to their rooms and sit just like they were sitting then, only without their straw hats: strange deep-sea divers, submerged in their own worlds. And the two women took Iboja's mother gently under her arms, placed her in the wheelchair and pushed her inside.

If your mother was a flower, she'd be a helichrysum. They grew by the fence in our garden and in autumn Mama would cut them and put them in vases. Such hardy flowers and yet lifeless—in fact, neither living nor dead.

Sára spoke to try to dispel the gloom as she helped Iboja push the wheelchair into the lift.

La vase . . . où est la vase, ma petite? Et la rose des rois?

The old lady's voice suddenly piped up as if a cyclopean eye had opened in her forehead and she could see more than the people around her. She turned her head to Sára, who after many years could now see her face clearly again. She looked like the trunk of an old tree exposed to intense heat, though traces of her bygone resolve could still be seen in the cracks of her face. Only her eyes could no longer cope. Looking at them was like jumping into an empty hole in the ground.

You can see for yourself what strange worlds she inhabits. You just can't get through to her.

Iboja was whispering, surprised perhaps, even fearful that her mother might somehow understand her.

The old lady was now standing in her room in front of the long rectangular glass of a mirror. One of her arms was stretched out to touch her reflection, reaching out to touch her fingertips in the mirror:

La couleur verte . . . verte . . . toujours verte . . .

She reached out her left arm, again touched the glass with her fingertips. She then tried to raise her arm but when she could lift it no higher, she growled angrily:

Merde! Merde . . . jaune . . . jaune . . . Je vous dis!

Iboja pulled her to the armchair and could only sit her down by forcibly bending her knees with her arm. Soon the old woman looked as if she was sleeping with her eyes open, lost in the deepest of dreams. But the nature of these dreams could never be known; they spiralled around in a hermetic vacuum within her. She had been thrown from the cliff of wakefulness but had not yet reached the silencing sea below, the mysterious element which swallowed up everything. Perhaps the film of her life was playing back to her over and again: the happy and comfortable flat in her parents' flat next to Aurora; her first love and marriage while still at university; the journey with her husband and the choir to Paris; the decision to emigrate. Then the struggles in her life: hunting for lodgings; mouldy Parisian flats; searching for work; finally, thanks to her father's contacts with the Russian émigré, finding work as a singer in the Star nightclub, then later the *Rasputin*; her husband's meaningless death; her thwarted wish to have Iboja with her; filling in applications, waiting in vain, later occasional visits from her daughter; then her barely perceptible drift into alcoholism, stupefaction of the senses, tablets; the feeling that she had a hole or a clump of cotton wool in her head; the madhouse in Paris; now this island, the final obstacle. Occasionally, scraps of sentences came out, weird words and one name which a reassuring voice uttered above her: Iboja.

When, before leaving, Iboja looked at her sitting mother for the last time, crouched down before her, squeezed her cold hands and rubbed them between her own, her mother did not even shift her gaze. She just fidgeted slightly in her chair and went on attending to the echoes inside and the shadows around her. Perhaps they still gave her a hint of some long-forgotten feeling of safety and security.

Iboja and Sára took the bus back to town:

Despite everything, I am glad to have seen your mother again after so many years.

Iboja nodded and carried on in her breathless way saying it was no wonder her mother's mind had finally gone. All those memories! Being cut off from everyone and everything! Perhaps the mind can be taught to switch off, who can say?! She'd not had it easy: after emigrating to France, she really wanted to have Iboja with her. Grandfather agreed but he wanted his daughter to go to Israel—afterwards, everything would have been easier to arrange.

But my father didn't want to leave Paris and go to Israel. And some invisible bureaucratic rules kept me here like a little hostage. After a few years in Paris, Father was killed by a car. He'd been sitting in the street with Mama, drinking coffee and was just crossing the street to buy a newspaper when it happened! He didn't look to the right and the car ploughed straight into him. Mama saw everything but still didn't come back—she stayed out there alone. Fortunately, she went on singing at that Russian cabaret—she thought she would be arrested here, just like her father was in 1953 for alleged embezzlement of property in his own hotel. We never spoke about it in our family—about his terrible end. It's rather like the death of your grandmother.

Iboja hugged Sára and continued with her torrent of memories.

When it happened to Grandfather, she already knew how to read. Her grandmother had left a copy of *Pravda* open on the crumpled lace tablecloth and she had noticed the headline: 'Thieves of Nationalized Property'. Through the closed bedroom door, Iboja could hear her grandmother crying. She threw her school bag on the ground and went on reading: 'Rudolf Štern, former owner of the luxury Hotel Aurora, is being investigated for not declaring silver cutlery, crystal glasses and porcelain dinner sets during nationalization. The bourgeois hotelier is also being questioned about allegations made by a waiter of him watering down bottles of vodka and *borovička* through their corks. After the investigation is finished, the suspect will be taken to the district court.'

Neither Iboja nor Grandmother, nor the faithful Auntie Zuzka, nor anyone else for that matter ever heard how the investigation was conducted, how the investigators shone a torch in his face, how they kept waking him up in his cell so that he couldn't get any sleep, how they kicked his game leg and accused him of faking illness to avoid having to enlist so that he could go on 'festering' in his cosy hotel with his family, how his one daughter went off on some decadent trip abroad and never came back. They kept swearing at him and calling him a grasping old Jew until he signed his confession.

Iboja, her head hanging down, paused for breath before whispering to Sára:

They walked him from the police station to the court in handcuffs. They did it as publicly as they could—walked with him through the centre of town at the very time when there were the most people out, as if through a guard of dishonour! Everyone knew him here and liked his cheerful personality. My poor grandfather could not bear it! He managed to free himself for a second and then leapt under a passing lorry . . .

Perhaps Grandfather could have refuted all the allegations; in court, he may have spoken so clearly and logically that they would have freed him. Sometimes one moment is enough, though. Such is fate. Something in Rudolf Štern must have snapped once and for all.

Didn't you know, Sára? He killed himself. Mama and Grandmother then both fell ill. Mama could no longer sleep and became more and more tired and haggard, started forgetting the words of her songs and had to see a psychiatrist. And Grandmother fell into a deep depression. I couldn't leave her here alone. Not even after August 1968 when I finally had chance to go and live with Mama for good. We went on meeting from time to time but neither of us spoke about me moving there for good anymore.

Iboja carried on with her reminiscences in her dry, matter-of-fact manner. She was used to it from her long conversations with herself at home, alone in her old age.

Once, during a visit, her mother took her to the *Rasputin*. Iboja observed the rich red and gold colours of the wallpaper and the panelling, the white and black tables with guests—mostly Russian émigré quaffing vodka and champagne, eating stroganoff and caviar and endlessly raising their glasses to grandiloquent toasts ... And up above a figure of the bearded Rasputin, with enormous cold eyes, watching over all of them! Iboja sang and danced in Russian folk costume the whole evening. Occasionally someone would grab her round the waist, pull her down from the stage, pour a shot of vodka down her throat or slap her behind ... She would then sleep the whole day, waking up late in the afternoon to put wet tea leaves on her swollen eyelids and eat what her daughter had cooked for her ..., then a shower, powdering, make-up and once more to the *Rasputin*. In the end, Iboja was happy to go back to where she felt more at home—and besides, her grandmother could soon no longer even walk. Fortunately, her old aunt, Zuzka, was able to help her. When the old woman died, Iboja's mother came to her mother's funeral.

And you were also there. A lanky eleven-year-old girl. You came with your mother . . . And my mother again said that she wanted me to go and live in France with her but it was too late by then for all that.

Iboja's mother was over fifty and starting to have the face of an alcoholic. Iboja finished her studies and started working in a museum:

After one long-distance relationship which went on for two or three years, I lived secretly, in my thirties, with a married man (I don't know if people gossiped about it around town). The marriage 'didn't work' or so he said. Apparently his wife was very ordinary with no imagination—I guess that's how he justified his behaviour to himself! They had children but I never wanted one. Children have to put up with a lot, often more than their bodies can bear, especially their inner selves. They can be damaged for life. So I never wanted a child!

Besides, Iboja only ever wanted a relationship where the door was open. As she told her lover: 'Such relationships are good when things break down, because marriage slams the door shut and digging a tunnel out calls for immense strength. Unless both spouses are so reasonable that one of them is actually willing to unlock the door . . .'

But I might be wrong. You live in Germany with your daughter and son-in-law—you've got a grandchild. Even though you're divorced, I don't suppose your outlook is as bleak as mine.

Sára was delighted to hear her grandson mentioned. It was a strange thing to her that, just five months before, Christian was still a moving outline in his mother's—her daughter's body, that he was just taking shape under her skin, and that now he could smile, stretch his legs and wave his hands around. It seemed like a miracle to her. She had started wondering what he would say first and then how he would describe his world to her and which words he would use. So far, he merely looked at everyone with those enormous black orbs of his; it was as if he knew everything and could see right to the bottom of things. Perhaps he was thinking: don't you understand me? Why not? I can see you perfectly! Those orbs of his were almost spilling out.

Yes, everything is easier for me than it is for you here. I still like my work—my pension can wait. I still love my test tubes and the smell of the lab—chemistry is such a great science, just watching molecules change is so rewarding. I love the beautiful structures, the models of molecules, the chemical bonds that form and their density of electrons. And when I look at people, all I see are chemical reactions.

And she laughed vivaciously.

Here in the real world, outside the lab, it sometimes all just seems like chaos and melodrama.

I'll show you a little drama. Come with me!

And Iboja took Sára by the elbow.

They'd just got off the bus and were taking a shortcut to the main street. The houses were brightly coloured and quite unlike Sára remembered them. They had always been grey, at best a dull ochre. Now they were wildly colourful, as if they had eaten magic mushrooms, she thought. The shop windows were full of Asian goods and there were 'English Second-Hand' signs all over the place.

This was the Czechoslovak travel agency where Mrs Bellová used to work!

Sára stopped in front of the house on the corner.

You've got a good memory! We both used to come here for German lessons. Then some fat woman, your classmate, I think, bought the house after inheriting a fortune from her parents. She lives off the interest on her inheritance, and, to fill her inner emptiness, tells people that they should forget about the old models of themselves and that medicine and vaccinations are a waste of time. She tells them she knows how to cultivate a radiant body, open your third eye, become clairvoyant, broaden your consciousness and work out strangers at first glimpse. The funny thing is she gave a pile of her own money to some similar charlatans who promised they could cure her obesity. I guess that's where she got her ideas from. So now, to try and get it all back, she's teaching her own transcendental mumbo-jumbo to old grannies in return for their pensions.

Both burst out laughing so hard that passers-by turned to look. They were now at the end of the old square—beyond were the high-rises of the housing estate. Iboja first showed Sára the remnants of the Hotel Aurora sign—only shallow relief remained. They looked up at the cupola in the middle of the roof topped by the figure of a woman standing on one leg like a ballerina and holding a torch in her upraised hand.

That was cast in Budapest and designed by a sculptor who was born here but lived all his life in Pest.

Iboja couldn't remember if she had already told Sára about it. The time had come, though, when every detail—even the tiniest was important. Perhaps such details would offer clues: some cipher or a secret code.

I once went into the cupola. It was after we had been moved out, a few years after Grandfather died. Grandmother was worried something valuable may have been left in the attic. It stank of old grain, mouse droppings and dust. I found some broken rocking roosters that I used to sit in, my old skis, some rusty skates and a number of dolls—some with hair and some without—made of precious rubber. How I loved them! Each of them was either my patient or pupil and had a name and life story I'd created for them! They wore clothes Auntie Zuzka had made for them. Oh, she was an angel in human form, disguised by her hunchback, the sort of person we say even little birds in the park would bring food for. She was clever with her hands and never in a bad mood. And so kind-hearted! Auntie Zuzka loved my grandmother and helped her with everything. She lived with us until Grandmother died.

Oh yes, I remember her! She once knitted me a scarf and bonnet. When I came to yours, she would bring me cocoa and sugar loaf. Or egg custard.

Sára recalled how lively and alert that tiny person with pale, thin skin and a hump on her back was, how she reminded her of some strange animal—a fish from the ocean floor perhaps. Her mother once told her that right after their wedding, Iboja's grandparents had adopted Zuzka as a little girl from the Betánia orphanage. Apparently she was the most forlorn of all the little girls there, crouching in the corner because of her rickety back.

Iboja recollected what she had seen on her exploratory journey into the cupola all those years ago. She wiped her face as if again feeling those cobwebs on it. Among all the junk piled up, there were miniature sideboards, tables and dinner services with cups and plates ... Iboja's most precious toys. But she turned her nose up at them at the time and didn't take one of those dirty cobwebbed dolls ... She felt like a young lady then and loved only books.

Let's enter paradise!

Iboja proudly tossed her head back and went in first.

On the left was our flat—our grandparents', I mean. You can remember it.

Piles of women's, men's and children's shoes, pumps, sandals and slippers could be seen through the open door.

Ugh! I hate that horrible chemical stink! It used to smell of coffee and brioche in here.

Sára grimaced.

It really did . . . Upstairs were the reception rooms. The first was that lovely plush café where music would always be playing, even jazz. While he had his hotel, Grandfather really wanted jazz, it was so good! That music coursed through your veins—really got the blood flowing. But the officials at the time were afraid it would start a riot, that it would shake people out of their dull subservience, so they ordered Grandfather to stop booking jazz bands.

Sára could also remember the café—it had been the most lavish public room in the whole town. What she now saw was like a slap across the face. First came the stink of those toxic chemicals, like in the shoeshop opposite; then, along the walls and in the space between, even hanging in the windows, were piles and piles of goods stacked up pell-mell: clothes, handbags, toys, pyjamas, stockings, sweatsuits—everything together. High up behind the old bar sat a diminutive Vietnamese looking down at the jungle of goods. Iboja led Sarah to one of the high arched windows and pushed away the clothes hanging there to see the view outside. Sára then felt a pull on her skirt; a little Vietnamese boy was standing there frowning and waving his fist. They shouldn't have moved the goods on display in the window.

Are you guarding Daddy's things?

Don't worry, little boy, we're not here for those. Don't be afraid of us.

The little boy stuck out his tongue and ran to his father.

Sára saw across the road a large carpark where the large house they would go to for German conversation lessons had once stood. Opposite was the Prior department store, still with the same name. The two cemeteries lower down had both disappeared. They were opposite each other, separated only by a road: one Jewish, behind a high wall; the other Christian flanked by a much lower wall. Now new buildings stood in their place, offices of the new system.

Where are the bones of the dead?! It's rather like those soldiers in the wood, isn't it?

And what do you think? If it wasn't so difficult getting up that hill, they'd be burying people today up in the old military cemetery. Business is business! Having money means success, no matter how you get it! That's the motto for our times.

That's terrible! It's just as well Father and Mother wanted cremating!

We'll have to have a cognac after all this—I could drink one straight from the bottle! I've not been here for years and am glad my grandparents never saw it like this! Then we'll go and see the mayor—we still have a little time. We'll ask about your villa and whether it can be turned into a museum. Or another insurance company, car salon, pub, carpark . . . the list is endless!

Shouldn't I leave the house to my daughter, or to little Christian? asked Sára unexpectedly.

Your daughter would have to start renovating the place soon because I can't watch over it forever. People will soon be taking it to pieces . . .

Iboja was thinking of those outside the system and how they were chewed up—or temporarily left to live wherever they could.

Such people needed old, abandoned houses for their own shelters. In time, the villa would collapse and weeds spread through it like cancer.

But would your daughter ever come here to live? Hardly, Sára.

Iboja went on speaking in a rather strange, derisive tone of voice:

Perhaps I'm just old and sceptical! An old cawing crow! But what is it we are living in here?! Can you feel it?

She did not say out loud, though, how everything to her seemed so morally bankrupt, how people had calmly got used to the world no longer being a safe place—anywhere. People were both afraid of capitalism which had mutated, as well as Communism which had long since mutated . . .

Just so long as people don't mutate, too, Sis!

That was what she said out loud—but Sára could make no sense of it.

Between times/fragment/1950

HANUKKAH

Imro. Provincial town.

At three o'clock on a grey December afternoon, the Hotel Aurora looked like an anchored ship. The day was thick with fog and the streets looked helpless and lost in space with familiar sights now unfamiliar and somehow hypnotically softened. Behind net curtains in the lit-up rooms of upper floors, human silhouettes shimmered among the China roses and palm leaves like huge swarms of insects, or figures in a laced shadow play of ghosts, occasionally raising their hands in secret gestures like Noh actors. Using the ashes from their stoves, the locals had made grey footpaths through the frozen snowdrifts, and on the main road was a huge pile of coal dust that labourers had unloaded with spades from the back of a lorry. Its grey-blackness contrasted with the whiteness of the town nestling between the whiteness of the surrounding hills; the world had turned flat and two-dimensional with no preceding process of disintegration. The street was deserted with only the occasional hunched figure appearing and disappearing through some gate somewhere, the creaking of which momentarily disturbed the silence. The groundfloors lay in darkness; it was a Sunday and all the shops were closed.

The ground-floor café of the Hotel Aurora cast out a warm light from its glass chandelier and small table lamps next to which stood little vases filled with helichrysums and larch sprigs. There was just one guest inside—Imro. Behind the bar, the waiter was polishing wine glasses with a cloth while the waitress painted her fingernails.

Imro liked the hotel and its café with its smell of old plush, smoke and the fading scents of the cheap perfumes worn by the women.

Imro had enjoyed sitting in the café since he started his studies in Prague. The hotel had been built in the nineteenth century during a period of industrialization, the confident locals having acquired new ideas of luxury and the energy to rebuild the old townhouses on the square which had been damaged by fire. At the back of these elegant new buildings, they built their workshops for the manufactory of leather, soap, woven goods, buttons, smoked meat and various other products. The hotel was built on the corner of the main street and a long sidestreet where mostly meat yards were concentrated.

He looked out through one of the café's large semi-circular windows and could see at the top of the sidestreet the long park-like garden and neogothic facade of a villa which had once belonged to the town's richest butcher and meat smoker, Edo Gallo. Alongside the avenue of lime trees with crowns covered in snow, the building looked almost black—as if scorched by fire. Imro liked the elegant garden, especially in summer when gentle winds would shake the leaves of the lime trees and the ash and oak alongside and create a never-ending music.

In the fading grey light, the fronts of the townhouses opposite, across the main street, also looked stark without the cheering effect which the sunlight gave to their stucco work. Imro sat in the plush armchair pressed to the window. Through the light hoarfrost on the glass, he saw a white emptiness—a town as if lying on its funeral bier. In the distance, the regular rhythm of rolling stock could be heard. Imro liked to go and sketch the trains pulling out from the smoke-stained station, moving with their hypnotic rhythm to better worlds perhaps.

Beyond the high arched windows, the silhouettes of men in sheepskin hats and women in Persian furcoats and hands in muffs of the same fur could occasionally be seen walking along the street together with children tugging sledges over the crunchy snow. Sometimes the bells of horse-drawn carriages could be heard; less frequently a car rattled past. Imro observed everything as he smoked his imported mild cigarette. It was a few years after the war and austerity was setting in but Rudolf Štern knew how to get them for him. He would also send a few packets to Imro's father who hadn't been to the café for years.

The freshly roasted and ground coffee on the marble table was of an equally high quality. Imro was convinced, for no logical reason, that all the changes meant to happen would come to this little town, tucked in between the mountains, later than elsewhere and more gently and comically. He based it on his knowledge of the local people. They were unrefined, knew how to quarrel and mistrust each other but, when it was necessary, could pull together and use their common sense. The effects of change would thus be like when someone's tripped over into a snowdrift and not onto hard concrete. Only his father was constantly afraid, and there was nothing that could dispel that fear in him.

We have to be quiet, Imruško, very quiet and not draw attention to ourselves. We can't let anyone notice us—we don't want anything else bad to happen! Don't believe anyone, Imrík! Not even from this new guard!

Thus spoke his father to him in hushed tones. And now that hush in his voice was stuck with him and he would never get rid of it. In the morning, he would shuffle to one of his old salons where they let him help out though the owner was now the production cooperative. By coincidence it was the very same salon which the previous regime had not aryanized.

Such tact!

And, unusually, the old man smiled. In the late afternoon, when he came home, he only left the light on in the room where they stayed—the rest of the house was dark. He ate little, so there was always something left over. Since Imro's mother's death, the old light, warmth and charm had all gone from the house. The windows were coated in dust and dulled the light even in summer. Nobody baked sweet-smelling cakes; nobody fried doughnuts or potato pancakes, nor roasted fish like the Gentiles did at Christmas; no one made Imro's favourite veal in aspic anymore nor badgered servant girls to polish the parquet floors, furniture and wooden staircase in the villa, to beat the carpets and run the freshly washed and starched tablecloths through the mangle . . . They had even had to wipe clean the palm leaves and all the other larger plants in the conservatory before the holy days. Neither the radio nor the gramophone played anymore; Imro neither sat at the piano nor took out his flute or violin. And Father seemed to have shrunk somehow; he never went to the synagogue very often before but now he hardly went at all—only for Yom Kippur, Rosh Hashanah and Pesach. During Hanukkah, however, in the Jewish month of Kislev, they lit a candle every evening.

Imro missed the smell of his mother's skin, her insistent voice, the plans she had to open a healthcare school in the town which had made both Imro and his father so proud of her. She was gone for good. And the manner of her leaving had left deep scars on Imro.

His eyes, used to deciphering forms in all things abstract, now noticed a burning sword in the hoarfrost like some fanatical vision of a holy martyr sleeping in a burning bed.

Then and meanwhile/fragments/

SCATTERED MOMENTS IN TIME.

From the memory of a provincial town.

Imro's father liked to go and play bridge with Pálka—another tanner and trader in fur coats and leather goods. Also with them were the procurer from the bank and the jewellery-shop owner, Feld. Pálka had brought the game from Poland, where he would go to trade his leather products. They also played games for money but the sums involved were small. Despite the times being turbulent, these men lived lives that were peaceful and dignified. Part of this meant not gambling; it was their duty to secure their futures and spend less than they saved.

Pálka brought a samovar from Russia and taught his servant how to make a strong brew and serve tea in the correct manner. And he drank it with stewed cranberries to which the housekeeper had added some quince and sugar beet. Their pantry was full of jars of the stuff.

When our Marka kills the goose, I'll invite you to the feast! he would say heartily to his friends.

The slaughter of the live goose took place in a huge tiled kitchen. Marka, the housekeeper and Mrs Pálková bought the goose at the market by the church. With neither blisters on its feet nor a blunted beak, the bird had all the best signs of youth. Marka sat on a stool in the middle of the room holding it between her knees; she found the hollow in its head, plucked a few feathers and with a sharp knife, slit the bird's throat before you even knew it. Her helper caught the blood in a basin full of cubes of knedle, then brought the iron so that Marka could flatten the goose feathers through a damp cloth before deftly plucking them from the bird.

There will be lots of portions—it was well fed, not just with oat-flakes but also with corn. I'm not lying to you! hollered the house-keeper joyfully.

Oh how the master will enjoy his goose liver with cloves!

Old Pálka was one of the biggest womanizers in town and at balls at the Black Eagle would say to every respectable adolescent girl:

I didn't know angels flew so low above the ground!

And to old matrons he would cluck:

Oh, where else have I seen those beautiful eyes?

In response to his blandishments, all women would turn into 'flowers of surprise'. Or so he would describe them to the men gathered at the bar, puffing on cigars and drinking cognac. They would laugh uproariously, as if for the last time, as if they sensed 'a dark Friday for gentlefolk' just around the corner, a new age with an international labour song, a class struggle like none before, model workers, three-year and five-year plans, enforced quotas, work collectives rather than private entrepreneurs and people both in the towns and the country living without the superstition and dogma of religion. But before any of this came, Pálka would tell Imro's father how he could remember hearing the singing from the neological synagogue as far away as the square:

'Lord, who shall abide in thy tabernacle?'

And he would sing it with a throaty voice, and repeat that Jews and Lutherans of the town had been like half-brothers for years and each had their fine temples, though at one time the Orthodox Jews prayed only in a rented room of a house belonging to a Lutheran locksmith at the bottom end of town. The Lutherans had learnt certain wisdom from the Jews: how money should not shout but merely whisper, for example, and that was something the Catholics would never understand.

Just look at the flashy vestments they wear and how they parade in them like Old Testament high priests!

And thus he would declaim theatrically—adding with pride how he was happy to send his daughter, Sonička, to the Jewish school because the old yeshiva had an illustrious past and times were changing. Girls needed to have a good education, as the ladies from the Živena association who would go on various women's trips to Pest, Prague and other places around Europe kept saying.

Imro looked out through the window of the Hotel Aurora café at the house on the corner. It only had one floor but it was large and was home to the Bellas, a prominent leather-making family. The house, directly opposite, had a high roof under which there had once been storerooms. There was no light in the windows. The family was probably gathered in the kitchen in the other wing with the oldest of them, 'the great traveller' as they called him in town, dozing in front of the crackling stove. As a tanner, he had enjoyed travelling in order to make business contacts. But he also loved travelling for its own sake. He had visited all the great cities of Europe, keeping detailed notes about the central leather market in Leipzig and the production of fish oil used for leather processing in Norway; in Trieste, from where he usually brought leather of South American origin, he would feel quite at home. But he also wrote about the terrible rumbling of Vesuvius, Raphael's paintings in Florence's Pitti gallery and about concerts and plays in London and Paris. The last long journey in his life was by train to Stockholm and then to Trondheim and then by ship (the Heinrich Wrangel) to the North Cape because he wanted to experience a polar night, that 'wonder of divine power' as he described it using an ink pencil he had to lick first before it would write. From there he went on to St Petersburg, Nizhny Novgorod, Kiev and Odessa, on to Romania and then to Bucharest before coming back home. He always took pride in bringing back the most expensive and best quality leather, not like other tanners who opted for the cheaper stuff of Poland and Galicia. He was perhaps over a hundred now, reflected Imro, beyond the reach of the outside world. He shuffled around his room, which felt like a museum to Imro when his father took him there as a boy. Bella did not even know that the large tannery, which he had equipped with modern machines and where he ensured his labourers had the same insurance and holidays as he had seen abroad, now bore the name 'Vesna National Concern'. In town, people would say that every Gentile needed his Jew to advise him just as every Jewish businessman needed his good Christian to smooth the path for him among the Gentiles. Such was the relationship between Imro's father and the much older Bella, and so it had remained till now.

If Imro's father ever went out on a Sunday, it was most often to see bald old Bella. They would sit in silence, each buried in his own inscrutable soul, and drink tea. Only Bella no longer had his in precious porcelain but in an ordinary earthenware mug because of his shaking hands and dementia. His daughter, Soňa, brought it to them, but she too was rather long in the tooth now. She had once acted in amateur dramatics, even properly kissed the male players because that was how the playwrights wanted it, though the ladies in the audience would gasp. They had also performed in an open carriage adorned with ribbons in the nearby villages, but the best was in the Black Eagle hall, on the big stage, where people would throw them packets of sugar as a reward when they bowed at the end. Soňa, apparently disdainful towards the local men, had never married, and now had to put up with her father's grumbling as well as those visions he had which made him shout and wave his arms. She had to lock his bedroom door, so that he would not set off on another long journey in his felt slippers.

In the frost on the window, Imro could now see white geometrical shapes clustered to form high buildings and chimneys.

Then/fragment/, 1939

BEFORE THE TWILIGHT OF THE GODS

Chimneys.

The Latin professor wrote carefully in tall Gothic letters SOL LUCET OMNIBUS on the board. The students had to put the verb into the perfect and pluperfect. It was an appropriate task—a war was about to start and the present tense of the verb would disappear in a hellish metaphor.

    Twilight of the Gods

    Twilight of the Gods

    Twilight of the Gods

    Twilight of the Gods

    Twilight of the Gods

    Twilight of the Gods

    Twilight of the Gods

    Twilight of the Gods

    Twilight of the Gods

    Twilight of the Gods

Ironically associating the sun and the life-giving strength of the Almighty, Imro suddenly scrawled down the words on a sheet of blotting paper. Together, they formed a chimney.

Then/fragment/, 1940

BLACK ON BLACK.

Ostracization.

An official letter from the grammar school came for Imro. It said he was forbidden to attend any secondary school, go to the cinema and library or walk in the park.

The people's louse-ridden state, the clerical republic, as they called it at home, wanted to rub him out and turn him into a butcher's apprentice. Instead of a chance to study, they would give him a wooden spoon to stir pigs' hearts, tongues, skin and the meat from their heads and knees in a huge cauldron in some steamy, white-tiled room where other helpers in white aprons would then slice up the congealed mass to make Gallo's famous brawn. Gallo said that such work was not suitable for a sensitive little boy, however, and then proudly declared:

And remember, we are not just common butchers—we are a caste, we are smokers of meat! We don't kill animals, we don't look at their hot blood—we *process* their meat!

So Štern, owner and manager of the Aurora, helped out again by arranging for Imro to be the official apprentice in one of the several fashion salons owned by his father. There, in the back room with a window looking out onto a bare yard where pigeons would flutter around in confusion, he had secret Latin lessons with the teacher from the gymnasium and was surrounded by books instead of fabrics, scissors, full-length winged mirrors, plush carpets and fashion magazines like *Hvězda, Jardin des modes* and *Chapeaux de Paris*. In the background was the hushed gossip of the female customers being attended to by the master seamstress, trying on new dresses. A Mrs Petrášová, who had once studied at a lycee in Nice and was wife of the town's best surgeon, went there three times a week to give Imro French conversation lessons.

Marienka, I will have the seamstress make you one of those dresses you liked so much—in dark-blue taffeta, if you remember, the skirt in four unironed pleats. It is the height of fashion in Paris, ruched around the waist, with a trim collar and a velvet ribbon below. It will be something to bring a smile to your beautiful face during these terrible times! How could a woman of your taste not delight in it?

And thus would Imro's father address his pretty young customers, with that new, rather guilty smile he had when he once brought into the gloomy room cakes from Linhardt confectioners for them both.

Other teachers also secretly came, and so Imro, in that dark, narrow room which no customer ever entered, continued his studies. In the afternoon, he would go to the station to draw trains, the smoky waiting room full of village women returning home from the market, porters crouching on the platform or standing by the low station bar where men would drink beer. With nodding heads, the town pigeons would beetle around their feet, looking for crumbs.

Then/fragment/, 1943

THE UNKNOWN GIRL.

Imro and the girl on the train.

It happened that one day several mysterious trains arrived—Imro called them 'black dragons'. The cattle wagons were sealed but arms were sticking out of their barred windows. The locals brought food to these trains in little knapsacks: bread, sheep cheese, *klobasa* and bacon, which they put into the outstretched hands. Only once did the railwaymen open the door of a wagon. The body of a man was carried out; he was choking, gripping his throat and gasping. Someone threw a knife out onto the platform. Blood was dripping through his fingers. Was it suicide? Imro quickly sketched the scene. And it was then he saw that face: a tender, hypnotic, unknown face with a mysterious air of fading away and becoming transparent. She was a girl of thirteen or fourteen, the same age as he. She even smiled and then waved her index finger at him, which he repeated after her. They smiled at each other—two children at play for a fleeting moment.

Meanwhile the police had arrived to quickly carry the injured man away. The wheels of the train then started to turn with a screech, and the unknown girl disappeared forever. Imro knew, though, that in his drawings he would never stop searching for that profile, the thick dark hair falling to her shoulders, the taut expression around her mouth, the pinched cheeks and those unspeakably wide eyes. Behind the girl, he had seen bent bodies, motionless, like a sculpture, a mortified mass of dark figures.

The magical face of the girl and the strangled voices coursed through his head for a while before imprinting themselves like an icon into his memory.

Then/fragment/, 1944

NIGHTS OF PLEASURE AND ANXIETY.

Imro, his parents and the pastor's wife.

Even though his father had lowered his voice, Imro once overheard him talking to his mother about 'nights of pleasure' in the Hotel Aurora.

According to the locals, these nights took place in the ochre-coloured Aurora from the beginning of the war to the end. Imro once drew the building with its opulent façade of Ionic and Doric pilasters and high arched windows which not even the houses of the town's rich could rival. In the middle of its roof was a dome on which a figure of the Roman goddess of dawn stood, holding aloft a torch as a symbol of the world.

Štern has to turn a blind eye to them if he doesn't want to get sent to a camp, said his father more loudly.

And what about us? What about Imriško? It's he who matters most! his mother retorted and all her repressed anxiety and help-lessness were passed on to Imro. They all felt it in their community.

I've talked to Guot, it'll work out. And please stop worrying, because you'll fall ill—your spirits will be exhausted. I've always looked after you, haven't I? Štern will also get a christening certi-ficate. It will be easier for him because he can become a Lutheran like his mother.

It's not about our religion but our origin, don't you understand? If it wasn't for Štern, they'd have aryanized another of your salons and taken our house. He can't hold out much longer, you know. He is not that strong! shouted his mother.

To Imro, they seemed to be speaking in riddles. By the weak light of the window which fell onto the little table and armchair, his father surprisingly started to read, *sotto voce*, from the Book of Job as if wanting to prove his wife wrong:

O that you would hide me in Sheol and conceal me till your anger has passed! O that you would set me a time and then remember me!

Guot was a Lutheran pastor, prematurely grey, with the reputation of a tolerant and good person. He could talk openly and kind-heartedly to everyone, and believers appreciated the way he never terrified sinners with talk of hellfire and perdition. His wife ordered from Imro's father men's suits of the latest fashion for herself, thus irritating the other pastor's wife as well as all the older matrons of the town. They would throw outraged and disdainful looks at her and her short wavy hair.

Oh isn't she just so . . . *sophisticated!*

And thus they would gossip over their Sunday afternoon cream slices and cups of coffee, recalling the sermon only so that they could then mention the pastor's wife.

If girls don't have their braids cut, they will remain chained to all the tired old conventions. Women should break free and be themselves, not just servants or jewellery-wearing mannequins.

So declared the pastor's wife, further provoking those wagging tongues. Apparently, she even wrote poems and articles for a magazine which came out in the Czechlands. She also played tennis, swam in the river, used a bicycle and smoked long cigarettes which she carried in a silver case.

Imro imagined nights of pleasure in which fat voluptuaries with red circles painted onto their cheeks like in Rubens' paintings cavorted on creaking beds with metal springs while drunken men watched on as the naked women's fat buttocks, breasts and thighs shook like aspic jelly. Imro could imagine them perfectly and would secretly draw women's faces with bloody mouths and kohled eyes, which he would show to Zolo under the desk at school.

When they were caught by the neurotic chemistry teacher, sidling like a spider between the serried rows of the physics and chemistry room, he caned their backs so severely that their eyes stung.

Then/fragment/, 1944

BURYING BONES.

On the run.

A late September evening; Gallo's shiny Packard trundled along a bumpy field road with Gallo himself, and not his chauffeur, quickly driving Imro and his parents to a village safely away from the German soldiers. Imro sat pressed to his mother's side. The skin on her neck smelled of vanilla and he remembered how she had been baking *challos* that day which still exuded a sweet aroma from the bag at her feet. On the backseat, she rested her cheek on the head of her fourteen-year-old son. Despite the numbness in her head from the days of tension and hurried packing, she felt a tenderness towards him which enabled her to breathe more easily.

About an hour later, they carried their heavy suitcases full of clothes and valuables into an empty house. The light, a dull grey-yellow colour, came from bare lightbulbs and everywhere hung the musty smell of unaired rooms. A tinsmith had been living here. In one room the beds were made; before their first night in that cramped place, Imro's mother gently caressed him:

Don't go having any bad dreams, my boy!

And in a half-whisper, smiling, she sang him a lullaby:

'Tum-bala, tum-bala, tum-balalaika.
Tum balalaika shpil balalaika.
Tum-balalaika freylik zol zayn.'

Around the house lay assiduously hammered pots and basins, with piles of them stacked up in corners. The house's new occupants had to move carefully so that the pots did not crash to the ground and make a din. They slowly learnt how to live there. When it was cold out, they heated just the kitchen, and, in the evening, the little room where they slept.

When the unexpected exchanges of gunshot began in the mountains and Germans came to the village, they had to quickly flee to another hiding place—this time a cellar behind the house of a peasant couple willing to shelter them. The old smallholder and his wife made sure they had enough to eat and gave them goosedown quilts and the sheepskins of their enlisted sons to protect them from the cold.

The cellar smelled of potatoes, root vegetables and earth. That first night it felt like a grave to Imro—to his parents, too, perhaps, but they did not speak of their feelings. Imro's mother could hardly sleep at all—for a long time she was gasping for breath and quietly groaning. When it was finally silent, Imro carefully went out into the night to look up at the starry sky.

Everything was blurred in his head: their town in the distance; the nearby mountains. They were entering the unknown. The world was sinking, drowning with the war and everything which had and hadn't happened. Only Imro remained together with the planet-filled emptiness above. The trees rustled in the autumn wind and it was like music to him. One day, he would play those sharp and hushed sounds on his flute, the sounds of trees indifferent to all things human and chaotic.

There was an orchard nearby but it was a smell of spruce, fir and moss which blew in from the nearby forest. At least that's how it seemed to Imro as his nostrils flared like those of a hunted animal.

He had left in their town house pictures to welcome the Nazis with: cuttings from *Slovák* magazine—with photos of Fascists and people's front leaders embellished with fangs and skulls instead of faces. He kept thinking of his room, their comfortable house, the well-kept flower garden with its gazebo, benches with armrests in the shape of snakes, the spacious conservatory where he liked to read. He imagined the whole town with its chatter and other noises. But the space in Imro's brain where all his desires and dreams were stored was getting narrower.

When for a few nights they were able to move back to the tin-smith's house, his mother came to him one evening. The autumn nights were mild—none of them dared think what would happen when the snow came. Imro squatted by a tree stump. His mother stood above him stroking his head as if it were an expensive vase and kissing his temples.

Imriško, I wouldn't mind leaving this place, you know. It's peaceful and the nature is lovely! And yet the country never really appealed to us. Your father and I are town animals! Cafés, concerts, theatres—that's what I enjoyed.

How do you mean, leaving?!

Leaving this world—forever.

Mamele! What are you talking about?! You were caring for the wounded at the Red Cross not so long ago and you still have that school to open! Have you forgotten all your plans? You keep telling me to make space for mine!

Imro tried to speak nonchalantly, as if over the cup of milky coffee they would eat their *challah* with.

One day the machine wears out, my boy, said his mother calmly. There's nothing you can do about it—that's how it's always been. Anyway, let's go to sleep—it must be very late. Come to your mum, my little cub!

But she sounded more ominous than cheerful, Imro later remembered.

Once after dark, the smallholder came to say that for a few days and nights they could not leave the hillside cellar and go to the tin-smith's place.

The Russians and our partisans have both left the village and the Germans are coming back. They say there's going to be a huge scrap in the forests—there's heavy artillery here. They reckon there are going to be partisan raids at night.

He brought them groceries and milk in a jug, along with empty buckets and another pile of mutton skins to keep them warm.

And then they lost all track of time. During the next few days, there were shots and machine- gun fire as the mountain shook with unearthly booms. To Imro, it felt like a requiem for all the undefinable beings and worlds out there. When they lifted the thick curtain to look out from their hole in the hillside, they could glimpse, through the thin spaces between the wooden laths, grey days with blizzards alternating with nights when the snow shone. Houses must have caught fire because there was a sharp smell of smoke in the freezing air.

After several restless nights, Imro finally slept harder than for a long time. He was woken by the touch of his father and his voice, cracking from the constant need to whisper. Unshaven with long hair and hollow cheeks, he looked, in the strips of sunlight coming through the small opening, like a wild, alien creature.

Where is Irma?

He corrected himself:

Where is Mama?

There was terror in his whisper.

I was fast asleep and heard nothing. When did she go out? And where to . . . ?

Imro was struck by the purity and freshness of the freezing air in his face when, hunched up, he stepped outside.

Ma . . . me . . . le . . . !

The wind picked up and ripped the syllables from his mouth.

You must not shout!

His father had run up to him, breathing heavily, and grabbed him by the shoulders.

In the morning light, there were no footprints in the snow— the blizzard at night had covered everything: 'A huge blank canvas ready to be painted red' flashed through Imro's mind. To the sides were snowdrifts like human forms, like rows of frozen and unidentifiable soldiers kneeling in white camouflage.

You run to the old couple. I'll go and look in the forest!

He paid no attention to his father's protests, to his croakily hushed voice forbidding him to enter the forest even though it was finally silent there.

Imro waded through the frozen snow.

The forest was unknown territory. Grenades and mortar shells from the long battles had destroyed trees, and in places only the burned remains of their stumps could be seen; elsewhere, falling branches were piled up on top of each other. In other places, the tree trunks had been scorched. The forest was as devastated as the cities.

It was as if someone had turned over a thousand graves and someone else now had to bury all the bones.

bury the bones,

bury the bones,

bury the bones,

bury the bones . . .

At another time, he would have written it in the snow with a stick as he had once written about the twilight of the gods at school. He pushed on.

The wind dropped. The silence hurt his ears and places deep in his brain.

Imro was surprised by how close his mother was, by how peacefully she sat on the pile of snow leaning back against an undamaged tree on the edge of the forest. Her eyes were closed and her face turned upwards as if she were listening to something; her headscarf had slipped down to her temples while her black hair, thick black eyebrows and the grooves under her nose were all covered by a film of frozen snowflakes giving her face a strange dreaminess.

That girl in the wagon had that same terrible gentleness, Imro remembered when he realized his mother was dead. Then he plunged to the ground next to her and roared unarticulated sounds into the snow, choking as he pummeled the snow with his fists. As

the snow blocked the air in his lungs, he felt something like pleasure; something had burst in his brain and he wanted to suffocate.
But then that ancient survival instinct rose up in him like in an
animal released from a trap. He raised his head to breathe in, turned
onto his back and slowly sat up next to his mother. She was still
sitting but now leaning towards him slightly.

Beforehand/fragment/, 1940–1950

CONFLICT, TIME, INSTANT FORGETTING.

Town—the garden of the dead.

The town was not bombed during the war. Some of the house fronts were struck by bullets, machine-gun fire and cannons of German soldiers firing on the Soviet forces—damage which the citizens of the town slowly repaired. But they did not agonize over it for everywhere was the grinding poverty which followed war. Self-preservation was more important than nice houses. Even those people who took great pride in their homes thought so.

In the heated café, Imro only needed to close his eyes and he could imagine all of them: families of factory owners, merchants, the odd successful artisan, doctors, lawyers, associations of different kinds—there was one in every building, the town was famous for it. The Orol gymnasium, for instance, with its sign above the door saying: 'Strengthen your muscles to serve your country!' But Imro, an ungainly boy, did not go to exercise at the local Jewish gymnasium they called the Makabbi. He knew that right next door was the Linhardt confectioners where they used to go for hazelnut gateau and where he would have hot chocolate in winter while his mother had milk punch. Lower down was the jewellers' and the former Baťa store now simply called Shoes, then a small drapers' where he would go with his mother so that he could then carry back to one of his father's salons boxes of Chinese silk, Indian brocade, cashmere, taffeta, English tweed, georgette, chiffon . . . .

Their quality could not be compared to the hard, stiff fabrics of today which encased a woman's body like tin. In the local state-owned textiles mill, they made them from sawdust—or so it was said.

There was a barber shop next to the colonial goods store with its alluring scent of coffee, then the window display of a bookshop before which Imro had often stood as a grammar-school student—occasionally buying a book with blue-leather binding and gilded letters on the cover. Hamsun's novel *Hunger* had affected him the most, and he would often repeat to himself the demand of the Norwegian author that 'literature should be a whisper of blood about the whisper of blood and the pleading of the bone marrow'. Imro would have liked to achieve that in his painting, which he continued with after the war. If he wasn't reading in the conservatory of their villa, he would take his book to the river on the edge of town. He sat leaning against a willow on the grass and entered its parallel world as if he were the shadow of the hungry young hero, the writer, also son of a tailor, experiencing the pure irrationality of mind resulting from the various degrees of hunger he was going through.

After the bookshop came the milliners, the men's and women's outfitters and then the haberdashers, where Imro's friend and classmate, Zolo, would go to see Želka. If there was no woman in the shop choosing buttons, elastic, thread and cotton for embroidering lengths of cloth to adorn their shelves at home with, Zolo would drag Želka behind the curtain at the back of the shop where she would pose for him as a model. His favourite pose of hers was when she stood to adjust her suspender belt.

Zolo was not lying; Imro saw those old charcoal drawings in his portfolio, when, after the war, they travelled by fast train to Prague where they both worked in painters' studios—Zolo a student of wall painting and Imro of so-called chamber painting. In the student hostel, he saw other drawings of her, a woman and not a girl, in a state of near nakedness; he soon knew her body almost as intimately as if he had touched it himself: her slim trunk, small breasts, broad hips and belly and that triangle of thick hairs beneath. Želka still worked in the shop, only the owner had now changed. The new manager, a former cobbler's apprentice from the suburbs, knew nothing about delicate women's goods but was happy to turn them over in his thick fingers.

Zolo showed the drawings to Imro and triumphantly sucked on his cigarette:

What about you, Imro, you lightweight! Still doing wagons and goods trains, dry trees, paupers, your parents praying, walls, craters? And now strontium shadows, too!

Zolo made the same comments in Prague but hugged his friend as he did so.

Imro inhaled on his cigarette and went on studying the layout of his town as if he had been commissioned to draw it: he looked at the county hall and Catholic church in the square and imagined, as in a soft-focus film, crowds of Catholic families entering this shrine of incense and myrrh. He visualized the golden light of its Gothic altars and the blue rays of sun coming through its stained-glass windows. He would be happy to sit there himself and admire the sweet faces of all the Madonnas but it was the synagogue, hidden behind the rows of houses on all sides, which was for his family. The Lutherans walked up to their church from the bottom end of town but that had no appeal to Imro. Their singing was too shrill and tremulous, though the strange language and complex syntax of their hymns intrigued him and suggested some higher spiritual poetry. Inside they had just one altar with an austere painting in the middle. He liked the symbolism of the well, the woman with the ewer and the bearded and long-haired Christ dressed in white, a man who had belonged to one of the tribes of his ancestors. The Lutherans could reach their church from the square via a narrow alley, only it was not always appropriate as there was a distillery behind the fence which emitted strong smells of alcohol (boys would go there and breathe in the fumes deeply as if they were opiates, absorbing them into their veins). Those intoxicating whiffs of liquor aroused young bodies, kindling in their bellies vague, teasing ideas and excitement. The front stopped there thanks to that liquor: the Russian soldiers drank themselves daft at that distillery and then passed out in sudden oblivion. They were later seen staggering around the streets while Germans fired savagely on the town from the top of a nearby hill.

Apparently a memorial pylon was soon to be built on that hill with a garden to dead Russian soldiers; their bodies were gathered up once the front finally moved. Imro had recently read about it in the newspaper and returned to the heated café of the Hotel Aurora with news all about it.

At the end of the café was a raised dais for a small band, and, beneath it, a round parquet floor for dancing couples.

How many bodies had touched and tempted each other on that dancefloor, shown their animal excitement and desire for some quick amour! Inhabitants of the town, ladies, young mademoiselles, some of the better prostitutes, parties of soldiers from one side or other, tired and scared to death just a few moments before and now consumed by the sudden waves of music, dancing, perfume and pseudo love. Bursts of laughter. Whispers. Chinking of glasses. A rustle of kisses in the dark, after Štern, the hotel manager, had deliberately dimmed the lights. Conflict, time, instant forgetting ... The singer's voice was suitably hoarse as she sang of death and passion; a drunk prostitute was undressing on the table as officers rolled down the silk stockings they had only just given to her.

I want you all, my sweethearts!!!

And the naked woman on the table smiled with a mouth like a carnivorous flower before bursting into tears:

And then you will kill me, kill me, kill me! she howled drunkenly.

Couples danced on the parquet, their bodies openly rubbing against each other; it was like intercourse through their clothes, exciting, musk emitting. Štern understood it and never tried to restrict them in any way. At least not for that one evanescent night. After all, at any moment, the long night might come for all of them.

Meanwhile/fragment/, 1950

THE FAIR-HAIRED CORPSE.

Imro, Aurora and those others.

Imro, who was still sitting in the armchair smoking, sipping coffee and reminiscing had not yet seen Štern that day. But he would surely appear at any moment through those swing doors, separating the corridor to the kitchen from the café, and say something like:

Imruško, my friend, have you come for Hanukkah? In a few years, you'll be a grandmaster! Will you paint my portrait, Imro? And one of my wife just as the Almighty made her? Because she can't do it very often anymore and I'm always up for it!

He would laugh uproariously, as always, even during the most terrifying times.

Those Heil-Hitlering Fascists in jackboots didn't break me nor will this new Klemo. They say I'll be able to go on working here in my own place, like your father. Ha-ha, what an honour! Do you know what those new shysters want, those old bricklayers and lackeys who don't know how to wear a suit nor knot a tie and are now all over the county hall? Apparently they want to turn my hotel, my good old hotel, hotel of the beautiful Aurora who has seen so much, into flats for the working class! But apart from those few parasites we've always had, we are all working class in this world. They'll do it over my dead body, Imro—I'll outsmart them, don't you worry. No one in this stetel can pull the punch I can! And money always talks!

He would say something like that in one breath; it was the same he had told Imro when he was home for the summer holidays.

Now Hanukkah was starting for just the few of those who were still there to celebrate it; the rest of the population were preparing for Christmas. But Štern's short rotund figure with its distinctive limp had still not appeared. Often when they were sitting alone together, Štern bent over to kiss the thigh of that lame leg:

If in 1937 Kuchárik hadn't been so cack-handed and had hit the deer instead of my leg, I would have been conscripted. I'd have gone to the Eastern front where the Germans didn't trust us anyway. I'd have faked deafness and they'd have put me in the kitchen! They'd not have had me! But home is home and the front is the front! Whorish wars—always one brewing while another breaks out!

Štern would talk about his lame leg and then mention the two gold canines in Kuchárik's mouth.

He'd show those off more than any of his others, the daft chump!

Imro closed his sketchbook, put his thick, soft charcoal pencil in his jacket pocket and stood up. The waitress smiled at him. She had only been there since summer; back then, Štern had told Imro she was a cuddly thing and the offer of a glass of port might persuade her to go back to the cold house where Imro lived alone with his father. Štern would give him a bottle of port—he still had ways of getting top-quality goods.

And I'll use them to catch all those new political shysters just like I caught all the old ones! The biggest scumbags in town have turned their coats inside out and will do so again when the time is right. The black shirts have now put on their blue shirts and play at being comrades, standing in the tribunes on 1st May and waving like children to the crowd that march by as if they'd been hypnotized, singing those infantile songs and waving their red sheets. And those pathetic floats showing agricultural scenes, classrooms and doctor's surgeries with those embarrassing living statues—oh dear me!

He would finish with a whisper, leaning over the marble table.

Imro took a small sketchbook out of his pocket and left the café, signalling to the daydreaming waitress that he would be back soon.

He then ascended the L-shaped stairway. It was covered by a threadbare red carpet with a simple Persian pattern woven with black and white cotton that had now turned grey. The carpet was held in place by brass stair rods, carefully polished as Štern always insisted. Imro had not been into the residential part of the hotel for a long time—he had no reason.

He went up to the first floor. There were probably no guests on the higher floors—few people travelled during those times. Old wallpaper in a golden-bluish colour with a Baroque cartouche had come unstuck in various places. It was the chambermaid's job to try and stick it back where possible.

Imro knew that it would be the right angle: a narrow space bathed in an anaemic winter light from the window at the far end, high doors made of solid walnut, brass handles and two figures—large and small—at the very end of the corridor. They would give the sketch its sense of solitude and vague anxiety. He made his first few strokes on paper. Then that small figure, a five-year-old girl in a yellow beret started to shriek:

Lollipop! Sausage! I want a lollipop! And a sausage! I want them now!

Be quiet! Be quiet!

A man, her father perhaps, slapped the child's head until the yellow beret fell to the red plush. Imro tried to memorize that expressive combination of colourful stains. Then the child threw herself on the ground, lay on her back and kicked the air with her felt boots trimmed with leather below and at the sides. The man dragged her by her leg into their bedroom, cursing as he opened the door. Imro stood at the other end of the corridor and was sketching the child being pulled by her leg when he heard a rustling noise behind him. Two men in leather coats and wide-brimmed hats came out of a room near to where he stood, striding out briskly, side by side, to the staircase. They were of almost the same height, and, in their identical clothes, looked like twins. One looked around, noticed Imro, put his hand in his pocket, stopped for a split second then moved on before disappearing out of sight. It was one of those sinister moments which Imro always had a nose for.

He ran back and knocked on the door the men had come out of. There was no reply, so he squeezed the door handle and entered the room.

A young woman was lying across the bed. Imro guessed she was young by the delicate body wrapped up in the velvet bathrobe and the long legs which stuck out from it. Her fair hair was parted down the middle, one side reaching almost to the ground and the other pressed into the pillow. He could guess her youth by the arm which hung from the bed, by her slim fingers and smooth skin. At the nape of her neck, where her hair parted, he noticed the belt of the bathrobe twisted around her throat. He shivered as if a blast of cadaverous cold had just blown into the room.

The floor was strewn with blouses, a folded skirt, underwear, fine stockings with a black heel and seam, a kind very difficult to come by, a sleeveless woollen lace plum-coloured dress with pearl buttons and gloves of the same fabric which would reach to her elbows; a dark-blue coat with a grey fur collar and a matching muff lay on the back of her armchair. Amid all the mess were sheets of music on one of which Imro noticed the song '*CIEMNA DZIŚ NOC...*'

He could smell moist air from the bathroom; perhaps the girl or young woman had just come out of the shower. She must have just dried her body, slipped into the bathrobe, undone the turbanned towel round her head and sat down at the mirror to comb through her thick fair hair as those two men had come in. Perhaps there had been a struggle or perhaps they had strangled her immediately before beginning their terrible search.

Imro was about to push the hair from her face and touch her skin when he realized with horror the danger of leaving fingerprints and then being accused of something terrible he had not done; such was the era. He would disappear into prison forever— perhaps it was a trap aimed to catch him. He looked at the dead body, still warm as if asleep.

He ran out of the room and downstairs in search of Štern so he could tell him there was a murdered girl upstairs and that he had nothing to do with it—that he was only sketching the corridor to capture the hotel's atmosphere.

Some more guests had come into the café but the two men in leather coats were not among them. Štern was neither at the bar nor milling among the guests as he liked to do. Imro turned, ran through the vestibule and rang the doorbell to Štern's flat opposite.

The servant let him in, the 'househelp' as such people were now called. When he ran frantically into the parlour, she called after him to say her mistress was lying in bed with a migraine.

Štern, Štern! he hollered and dashed into the bedroom without knocking. Štern's wife was lying in bed with a compress on her brow. On the adjacent bed a little girl was sitting, sucking her thumb and picking her nose. It was Iboja, Štern's granddaughter, and Imro tried to appear calm with her there.

Oh, Imriško! Is it you?! I didn't know you had come home for the holidays ... How is your father? This pounding in my head will drive me mad! groaned the woman plaintively.

The little girl took her thumb from her mouth and wide-eyed, announced how a bear had got up from the floor in the night and wanted to bite her—and Grandma, too, though she had been snoring, and how Grandad was sleeping in the next room and the bear was afraid of going up to him.

She wouldn't let me sleep a wink. I had to take both the bearskins away. She's always been scared of those heads and teeth. It's pointless telling her they were shot in the forest long ago and are here to keep our feet warm when we get out of bed. I just wish that drilling in my head would stop! Do you think that little one has inherited my congenital sadness? My husband thinks it is just boredom I suffer from but what does he know?

Imro leaned over the little girl in her long nightie and took her in his arms. He then carried her to the window, pulled open slightly the brocade curtain drawn shut to keep out all the light and showed her the circle of snow-covered silver spruce trees standing in the garden.

Beautiful, aren't they? And so quiet. Look at them in the evening when the moon is shining. There will be a magician standing there

sprinkling them with diamonds—magicians love sprinkling diamonds just so they can make little girls like you happy.

To him, though, the garden looked like an old woman who had
lost her memory; withdrawn, freezing and passive—like a dead fish.
There were no visible traces of the cultivated lilies of various colour
and species, of the dahlias, phlox, petunias, slipper orchids
and begonias among which Štern and his wife would drink chilled
wine on wicker chairs and tables. The wild rose bushes looked like
savage monsters.

Never be afraid of anything! Never! You're a brave little girl,
Iboja, and always will be!

Imro smiled at her and tickled her nose with his finger.

She smiled back, leaned her head against his throat and again
started to suck her thumb. Once he had drawn the curtain, he put
the child back on the side of the bed where Štern would sleep when
they didn't have their daughter's child with them.

Where can I find Rudo?

Štern's wife merely shook her head, waved her hand and groaned.
He went out of the room and realized his panic had subsided.

He went back to his table in the café and decided to wait there
for Štern, who would then call the police. He himself could not
nor could he say that he had been in the room of an unknown
woman. No one except the faithful Štern could know about it! For
Štern was a master of the art of living and knew a way out of every
situation. He was always cheerful or at least could pretend to be;
he could get through to everyone, get them all on his side.

At last he saw the small, round, slightly limping figure of Štern
with his reddish beard and thick wavy hair smoothed back with
walnut oil.

Imriško! My friend! Is it the five-year plan calling? Welcome home!

Štern greeted him histrionically and held out his hands as if he wanted to hug a little boy. Imro grabbed him by the lapels of his jacket, sat him down next to him and feverishly related what he had seen in the bedroom upstairs. Štern narrowed his eyes and was grave and silent for a moment but when Imro started to insist on him calling the police, he quietly tried to persuade his young friend, the son of this old friend—why Imriško could even be his son if he had started with sex sooner!—that he was seeing things, that the whole film scene he thought he had witnessed was just a figment of the sensitive imagination of this great, famous artist-to-be, this future gift to the world from this crumby one-horse town. Even the name of the song was cinematic. '*Ciemna dziś noc!*'

Isn't the song in that melancholy Soviet war film called *Tomnaja noc*?

And Štern continued in his flamboyant manner, even singing some of the melody sung by the soldier on guitar in his dugout, his eyes gazing dreamily along with those of the other soldiers in the hole during a break in the battle. And then he went on briskly:

*Two Soldier*s is on at the cinema—it's so sad and moving and they're showing it together with *The Fall of Berlin*. Not long ago they had another sad one on—*Wolf Holes* with the pretty and mysterious Magda Husáková-Lokvencová playing alongside Bielik . . . .

And he went back to Imro's fear, claiming that it was small wonder he had such visions given everything he and his parents had gone through during the war! It was all the worry and anxiety that was to blame. Guot, the pastor, had been willing to christen them if they had wanted him to. But either they didn't or there hadn't been time before the Germans came. And then there was that terrible hole in the ground, his mother's death, the fear which had become his father's second skin.

So Imro, it's no surprise you seeing things! You've been through hell and now those demons want to drag you back there. But you're strong and you can't let go. You're not depressed, it's grief which you have and that's good. Don't mistake deep grief for sadness and depression. Depression is really bad, a rebuke to the Almighty for not giving you what you want. But when you are downhearted as you are, you are like a child who is crying because his Father is a long way away. These are the wise words of Rabi Nachman from Vratislav, you know?

Imro angrily interrupted him:

If you don't do it, I'll go myself! Štern, didn't you invite a singer from Warsaw for your Christmas concert? You go there with old Gallo just to relive your old business trips. Or from Zakopané! You've always had a soft spot for Polish blondes with their special charms and their lisps, you've always known how to put on a show, you've never wanted vulgarity or those new songs with their fatuous lyrics, like that march I hear in the capital every day from the speakers: 'We're all young, you bourgeois Westerners, even Comrade Staaaaalin! . . .' You want the old melancholy and passion, you want people on your hotel's polished dancefloor to feel the old subtlety. Just admit it to me, Štern! I won't want anything more from you, I won't sit here or in your home if you don't report the murder and those men in leather coats . . .

That's enough, Imro! Come with me!

Imro was soon out of breath and coughing so quickly did they run upstairs. Štern unlocked the door which Imro had slammed shut just an hour before. But now the made-up bed was empty and the clothes had all disappeared. There were no sheets of music on the table beneath the mirror, no steam from the bathroom; dusk was creeping in through the window—these were the shortest days of the year. There was not a trace of violence in the room only an impersonal emptiness, the gloom of an unoccupied hotel room. Nothing else. NOTHING!

Štern, you know I'm not losing it—not yet! She was here. She lay here . . . May I have a look at the guest book?

By all means! But you'll find no Polish girl in it, I guarantee you. Perhaps you've seen a play—some strange, bizarre play. But now we should both come down from the stage!

So tell me, was the murder to do with the new regime? asked Imro when they were sitting in the café again.

Oh, please! You didn't see anyone there! You weren't even in the room and there has been no murder! You were just seeing things! You're being as hysterical as my wife! The only people who come here from Zakopané are horse smugglers! And it'll soon be curtains for them the way the black market is being squeezed . . . Exports are ending and our shops are filling up . . . Customers fight to get in now when Baťa gets a new delivery. It'll soon be like in Budapest with its full window displays! No longer will our comrades from the villages have to take quilts with them to keep warm in the spa hotels! And there will be no more skimping and saving in hotels, you'll see!

As if to prove it, he clicked his fingers, made some signs and a moment later the waiter brought two glasses of port. Imro held his head in his hands and the idea came to him of him doing a self-portrait in that pose. It would be green-yellow and rather like Filla's *Reader of Dostoevsky* . . . He remembered Iboja and how she was afraid of those bearskins on the floor, their mouths wide open. He would draw those great orifices too, and even mentioned it to Štern, who again burst into such booming laughter some of the new café guests turned to look at him.

I shot one of those bears myself! Then the innkeeper's wife in the village roasted the paws . . . It's quite the delicacy! And she sang '*Limbora, limbora . . .*' and to this day I don't know what kind of tree it is and what kind of nuts fall from it but I've taught Iboja the song . . . You see! You've loosened up now, you're no longer so uptight. Your vocation is art—that's your *raison d'etre*, as Marienka, the surgeon's wife, always tried to instil in you. And what a bear he is—a great surgeon, crosses himself like a good Catholic before every operation and none of the comrades dare say anything to him! Or—*ars longa vita brevis*! Isn't that what your old Latin professor taught you in that backroom of yours? We old guard will help you with the rest, fear not!

The scent of spruce sprigs and their resin broke through the smoke of the room. Imro could also smell the wind coming down off the mountains. He felt giddy from the port, the warmth of the café and the recent shock. His nerves were frayed.

The guests, the smoke, the chatter all increased. Everything now seemed indistinct to Imro; he would let some time pass—it flew past so quickly anyway. The truth would come out at some point or be buried even deeper! He pictured the fair hair across the woman's face which no one would ever see now as well as the face and dark hair of the girl on the open wagon and tears came to his eyes. But Štern was wrong: art was not about living in some ivory tower. His journey would take him across all the battlefields a person could imagine and either save or destroy him. The main thing was to keep one's integrity and want the truth.

I don't want to be guilty of anything either as a person or an artist! he muttered.

Oh my friend—you guilty? You are the purest of the pure!

The two men embraced and drank more glasses of port. And then Štern said:

The war is over and the world just wants to get back to normal so that people can again travel, study, paint, sleep, love and even kill themselves in hotels! It was always thus! And they will dance in coffee houses ... But things will never be as normal as they used to be, my friend!

With elbow on the table and hand on his forehead, he then said with a half-smile:

My wife bought a women's magazine the other day. What can I say, Imro! There's an article about some woman called Praskovja Malinina who's able to milk up to 60 litres a day from the cows of Kostromej! And there's another called Matrena Timoševová saying: 'I'm sitting in a dazzling marble hall listening to Stalin's speech and thinking: is it a dream? Stalin mentioned my name and I made him a promise that I would organize a women's tractor brigade.' So you see where we're heading, Imro! We even have model women workers here at the Matadorka plant!

The port was as thick as valerian cordial and soon the tears had stopped forming beneath Imro's eyelids.

Meanwhile/fragment/, 1950

J'ATTENDRAI.

Iboja, her grandparents and dancing in a circle.

The little girl was still sitting on the bed looking sleepily at the curtain behind which the daylight was fast fading. Her grandmother slept alongside, occasionally groaning, throwing out her hands, tossing and turning. Iboja was sucking her thumb again and picking her nose with her index finger. Then, first making sure there was no spreadeagled bear with big head and bared teeth on the floor, she tiptoed barefoot across the polished parquet to the window and pulled back the brocade curtain. She then pressed her mouth against the glass and with wide eyes looked down at the garden swimming in a dark-blue light. Iboja remembered how Imro had held her here and spoken about a magician and some extra diamonds he had just for little girls like her. The snow on the eight silver spruces in a semicircle, on the bushes and the bare patches in the garden twinkled in the light of the moon and the streetlamps peeping over the stone wall. Iboja so wanted to see that magician scattering his iridescent dust around the garden like a net. Her heart was beating with excitement but perhaps she was too late and had missed him.

Instead, two dark men in hats emerged from a door in the wing of the house through which hotel guests in summer could go out to sit in armchairs, drink coffee and smoke. The men then put something down on the snow-covered footpath which Iboja recognized as the carpet from her grandparents' parlour that the cleaner sometimes took outside to beat. Auntie Zuzka, who helped her grandmother with all the work around the house, was now too crooked and frail for such strenuous tasks.

The men bent down and again took hold of the carpet before walking to the metal door that led out through the garden wall. The whole scene was over in just a few moments and Iboja frowned, unhappy that she hadn't seen the magician in his starry cape and pointed silver-paper hat—the bearded garden gnomes standing at the corners of the garden and grinning at her were little consolation for his absence. Someone then knocked and Iboja ran to the bed to hide under the blanket. She heard her name whispered: it was only Auntie Zuzka with two mugs of cocoa. She put one down on Grandma's bedside locker, then pulled back Iboja's blanket, tweaked her nose, pointed to the half-open curtain and put the mug in her hand. The cocoa smelled sweet, the ceramic warmth heated her cold little fingers and something vague, obscure and dangerous which the little girl had momentarily felt in her mind now faded. Only something kept making her grandmother shudder in her sleep and throw her hands up into the air. The little girl was nodding off, though, when her grandfather came in with a bang and started singing:

'*Es singt meine alte gitare . . .*'

He sat on the edge of the bed and put his left hand under the head of the restlessly sleeping woman. She half-raised her eyelids and then shut them again. Beneath the blanket, her whole body tensed up.

My darling! As lovely as Rosita Serrano . . . ! So get up, it's almost evening and then it will be night . . . and again you won't be able to fall asleep! Smile. Look what I have for you—a sterling silver watch.

And he placed the small wristwatch on his wife's lips. She jerked her head away angrily and the watch slipped down on to the bed like a silver snake.

Iboja knew the Rosita record. There was a photo of a woman with a guitar on its cover. Her shoulders were bare, she had carmined lips, narrow eyebrows and long, curly eyelashes. When her grandad wanted it, Iboja would put the record on the shiny walnut gramophone in the parlour and the room was filled with its sound: '*Es singt meine alte gitare*'.

Now this is hard work for both of us—don't think it isn't! But we'll find you the best doctor—even go to Berlin if necessary.

And he ran his fingers through his wife's bedraggled shoulder-length hair, damp with sweat.

In Berlin we'll get you a new hairstyle with those big cold-waves as they call them! The Berlin hairdressers are the very best there are! You'll be beautiful and irresistible again.

I'm afraid!

And lying on her back, she pushed his head away.

Oh come on! It's only fear that frightens you! There's nothing else to be afraid of. As long as I'm here with you, we can get through everything!

So what are they shouting out from the loudspeakers? Those people who don't understand the new age with its two-year plan, three-year plan, quotas, joyful worksong and joyful struggle of joyful new proletariat, blah blah blah—such people don't belong here anymore! So where do we actually belong? Where!? I could spew on the whole lot of it! *Scheisse*!

Between her bursts of speech, Grandmother's crying got louder and louder. Iboja leapt up, grabbed a pillow and threw it at her grandfather's head.

Go away! Leave us alone! she shouted at him.

Surprised, Štern tried to speak to her but Iboja pressed her hands to her ears:

I'm not listening! Not listeni-i-i-ing! she yelled.

Meanwhile Štern's wife ran to the bathroom. In the mirror she saw her bluish complexion, sagging cheeks, puffy eyes and drooping mouth. And in one movement she threw to the ground the expensive *Guerlain* perfume her husband had bought her a year before on the black market, her *Palmolive* lotion and soap, jars of *Kaliopé* face-water, *Royal Ambré* face mask and *Sahara* suncream from the previous summer—the tiled floor was soon littered with her cosmetics. The sunlamp in its wooden box which he'd brought back from a business trip to Leipzig also got the same treatment.

What should I do with myself? I can't cope anymore!

She was clasping her head because the din in it was worse than those new brass marches blasting out from the speakers in the streets, filling the town like an invisible army, erasing all things old and rotten. She was afraid of those clamorous marches and the collective force behind them just as she had been afraid a few years before of those noisy marching songs with words like 'Guardist, be willing to lay down your life'. The most frightening for her was 'We're Slovaks from birth', a menacing song about axes and knives, about chopping and cutting and blood, sung by men in black uniforms who marched through the town shouting out slogans and then had drill practice in a nearby wood, on trampled pine needles, in a place where the townspeople had once had May balls and danced beneath trees decorated with ribbons and little lightbulbs.

Her husband still didn't know that her daughter and her husband would not be coming for the Festival of Lights—and that now they would never come home. She would not return from Paris where she had gone to sing with her university choir. Her husband had gone, too—they both worked at the law faculty—a short letter had arrived from them two days ago. But was it any wonder?! During the war, members of the people's guard had scrawled: 'Bigshot Jews—march to camp!' on the door of their flat. And a moment later, they had yelled beneath their window: 'Play to me, Pipe to me March! March! March!', one of the popular Fascist songs of the day! They wouldn't let Štern run the hotel for much longer; they would have it sold for scrap. They'd made old Beňadik—parasite they called him—stand in shame at the counter of the Cheap Goods shop or whatever it was called. He wouldn't speak to anyone there. And where would she go? Where, as a bourgeois madam, would they stick her? But worst of all, what would happen to that innocent soul—their little Iboja? She'd be hounded out of society just as they'd recently been! Her husband could do nothing about it—he didn't have the money to buy their salvation from the new powers-that-be, even if, as was said, those powers were made up of the same dim-witted and worthless people as before, only wearing different colours now and with different legitimation. What with the whiffs coming from its old leather works and soap factory, the whole lousy town stank in more ways than one.

They won't leave me anyone to help here, perhaps not even Zuzka! They've only left her here this long because we took her from the orphanage when we did and brought her up as our own. Or they'll send both of us to work the machines in Štalmach's old textile mill?! Perhaps they'll put Zuzka into a workhouse, they won't care that she's rickety and hunchbacked.

Her husband put his arms around her shoulders and led her back to the bedroom. Then through the open door to the parlour, he shouted:

Zuzka, a teaspoon of sugar and forty drops of valerian.

Zuzka had anticipated it and was already standing by the bed with a silver spoon, giving her mistress the panacea which would restore some calm. She offered to bring her a piece of roast turkey left over from Sunday as well as some buttered brioche she had baked freshly that morning to have with coffee. The troubled woman had to eat properly to get her strength back.

Iboja again burrowed under the quilt, imagining that she was a rubber doll in a pink cotton dress like the one Auntie Zuzka had crocheted, covered with that glistening veil in the garden, listening to the snow falling on the fir tree, the silver spruces and the bearded gnomes. But a moment later, she shivered at the idea and just as it had entered her head, so it went out. Instead, she recalled how her friend, whose mother sold hats next door to the hotel, told her that when winter was over, there would be a children's flower parade in town and that every child should wear a special flower costume for the occasion. Iboja wanted to ask her grandmother what kind of flower she could be and pushed the quilt from over her head.

The nightlamp was on and in its light her grandmother's face had a goldish hue while her grandfather's beard looked redder than ever. He was bent over his wife and they both spoke in whispers, though Iboja could often hear her mother's name mentioned and words like 'Paris' and 'escape'. Her grandfather looked very old and worn out. He was saying how fortunate it was that their daughter knew languages and could sing like a nightingale. He didn't really blame her, though she should have told him before: he could have arranged for Iboja to go too, but now she was like a hostage. And her grandmother said that she wasn't angry with Iboja's mother, only that she would like to be there with her—and with Iboja and with him. After all, the wife of the owner of the old textile mill had gone to a spa in Switzerland with both her sons—Štalmach had recently shown her a postcard of the Hotel Splendide they were staying at. They were keeping well, bathing in the pool, listening to jazz the whole time. And here? She had read in Slovenka how 'our women', Slovak women who went to spas, complained about that awful jazz being played in hotels and swimming pools rather than melodious Soviet or Czechoslovak songs . . . They will soon forbid him to have jazz bands playing in the hotel café . . . It was still possible to arrange a lot of things, though—that stupid new system was still rocking like a little boat on high waves but it would change and get worse, she could feel it . . . He should sell all her jewels and give up everything—just so long as they could all get away and remain together! Grandfather mentioned the *Rasputin* club and the Red Star—his brother in Prague, a pharmacist, once said he knew someone there. The old Russian émigré could help their daughter—there was a strong community of them there and she sang so sweetly. She could learn Russian and played the piano; and he knew how to handle the people here—one good turn deserved another and all that. It was the same under every system. But the best would be if they left Paris and went to live in Israel.

Suddenly they both went silent and all that could be heard was the ticking of the Swiss carriage clock which had been uninterruptedly striking the hour in its thin silver tones for decades.

Iboja was woken at night by a faint crackling sound. She recognized the music, the lisping voice. Alone in bed, she got up to look through the glass door of the bedroom and saw two dark swaying figures. She opened the door. Her grandfather was embracing her grandmother, now wearing a lilac silk shirt with orange polka dots. A lamp with a pale-yellow shade was lit; the girl could smell the cooked meat which she saw on a plate on the round table with the crocheted tablecloth. A record was playing; its cover, with 'Tino Rossi' written on it and a photo of the singer, was on the floor. When Grandad played the record, the singer always reminded Iboja of her grandfather even though he was clean-shaven and his voice sounded to the little girl like that of an affectionate woman.

J'attendrai
Le jour et la nuit j'attendrai
Toujours ton retour
J'attendrai'

Iboja had the impression that her grandma was crying again as she danced because her body was quivering but she couldn't be sure—perhaps, she was laughing; her face was pressed against her husband's shoulder and Iboja had never seen him so red in the face.

Perhaps Grandad's got a temperature, she whispered compassionately into the glass.

Her grandfather gently turned his wife around the carpet, kissing her hair by the temples. Now Iboja could see clearly that both were crying, both shedding tears, their voices rising to a wail which drowned out the music. It must have something to do with her father and mother, she decided, furrowing her brow and pursing her lips. She felt anger and fear scratching in her throat and slammed the door shut.

Through the net curtain she shook her clenched fist at those gnomes with long beards who crouched in the corners of the garden and had brought something bad and very dangerous to their house. She never saw again, though, those two men in hats and raincoats who carried that rolled-up carpet through the snow-covered garden.

Meanwhile/fragment/, 1950

WHEN MY LIFE ENDS, DEATH WILL END WITH IT.
IT WILL NOT OUTLIVE ME BY AN HOUR.
The Beňadiks.

Five o'clock sounded from the clocktower on the old county hall, now the national committee building. It was already dark, the streetlamps throwing yellow cones of light on to the creaking snow. Unusually there was no wind blowing from the mountain. Imro, however, his face burning from the shock, the wine and the warmth of the café, could not stop shivering. But he was not yet ready to go home, to his increasingly silent, prayerful father who had lit another candle to the *gabbai*. On his way home, he would stop at the Beňadiks, who had been living for a few months in one of the tenement blocks near the leather works. They had received a flat from the state after the new regime had forced them out of their manor house and seized their extensive gardens, woods and fields.

In all the shop windows was the same picture of a fir twig, a glass bauble and a burning candle—and above it, the words 'Peaceful Christmas'. Only at the corner of the square was a huge board with a longer message written on it: 'We are building our country through work and by working for our country, we work for peace.'

It was dark in the archway and there was a smell of potatoes and coal coming up from the cellar. Imro had only been to their new flat twice and had to grope around blindly before managing to find the spiral staircase up to the gallery. There, the moon and snow on the metal banister rail would at least give some light. He knocked at the first door and Beňadik opened it.

Servus, Imriško. Eliška and I have been waiting for you.

I got held up in the Aurora.

The old and young man shook hands and half-embraced.

Štern likes to keep you, I know.

In the living room, one could feel their forlorn efforts to recreate in miniature the opulence of their old salon with its expensive fitted furniture and fine carpets. Beňadik was in a brocade dressing gown, a snuffed-out pipe between his teeth. Eliška seemed even smaller than in summer, when Imro and his father had helped her arrange the furniture. She put down the bowl of baked apples she was carrying on the table and embraced her former flute student.

How handsome you are, Imriško! Prague obviously suits you! But nature is so unfair! It gives men their flawless complexion but look at me—old crow that I am! Just one big liver spot.

At the same time Eliška clapped her hands as she always did when he had played well to her. Her once elaborately coiffured chestnut hair was now grey and cut short—she looked like a mysterious foreigner. And she had shrunk somehow, and her face and the back of her hand were covered in brown patches. She sensed what Imro was thinking, and, when the two were sitting alone, her husband having gone to fetch some hot pálenka sweetened with caramel and sprinkled with crackling, she cheerfully said:

When my life ends, death will end with it. It will not outlive me by an hour.

94

I can tell you something on that subject, added Beňadik, pouring hot alcohol smelling of cloves and caramel into cut-glass tumblers.

In the morning, I went down to the cellar with the coal scuttle and . . . you won't believe it! The janitor's old mother was hanging from the ceiling. I grabbed hold of her legs and kept yelling out her son's name until he showed up. Between us we saved the old woman's life . . . She's over ninety and says that she doesn't want to live anymore and that God has forgotten about her! You see what's happening! People are losing their appetite for life and want no more of it. But let's not speak of death! Tell us about your life out there—about your studies, about you and your father. He doesn't visit us anymore—we never see him.

And he topped up their glasses.

They sent me to work in the Cheap Goods shop but I shan't let the idiots turn me idiotic. Do you know what they're doing? Putting up photos of the new guard to fill the empty places left by the old ones they took down. Of course they have the same half-witted faces! And don't we know how brave all these great comrades are! Oh yes, just as we know how they quickly changed their coats when the time was right.

Eliška slid the tray of vanilla rolls towards Imro:

And I was trembling all morning after what happened in the cellar. Imriško, please—help yourself! This year they're without bacon rind—better on the waistline.

She herself took only a baked apple though she didn't eat it but said how she had wrapped up some vanilla cakes for Imro's father as well as the little imps which she always made for children on St Nicholas' Day. Imro remembered them from his childhood. Eliška would put dried plums on cocktail sticks and then make the eyes and horns from bits of red apple peel.

No little children come here anymore so I've only made the imps now—just for us old people, your father included. And I've put some of the hot toddy in a little bottle for him.

The conversation was slow because Imro was reticent and unsure whether to speak about what he had seen in the hotel bedroom. But then Beňadik himself began a surprising tale:

Imrík, something's going to happen! Something unpleasant is in the air! The war and all that other madness—it's not enough for them . . . Father Guot called me. Apparently some secret policemen went round to see him and started turning over the whole place. They were alleging that some Polish spy in contact with the German secret services had been there. But his wife threw them out. I can just see it! Her hands on her hips and a cigarette in her mouth, she blew smoke into their faces and told them she was going to write an article about their visit and send it to the newspaper in Prague she works for. She said she wanted all the information and evidence they had, otherwise she would sue the intruders for falsely accusing her husband—a popular and highly respected figure, of hiding a suspect and collaborating with a Polish-German spy. The terrified cops left with their tails between their legs. But what's next, Imro? And what's behind it all?!

Imro vividly recalled the musical score in the hotel room and the title of the song 'Ciemna dziś noc'.

I don't want to hear about it anymore! My only priority now is peace! They've taken a huge part of our life away from us, that's what they've done.

There was anger in Eliška's words. She got up from the table, took from the case the separate flute parts, screwed them together, ran her fingers over the open holes, seemed to look out through the curtains with orange tree leaves and started to play Debussy's 'Syrinx', a piece she had taught Imro right after the war.

Timelessness began with the melody. Or was it a confluence of times? Everything happened at once and everything coalesced in a clarity of thought and senses. Imro's sense of self dissolved. But that feeling was discouraged at school. Instead, the students were taught the need to remove formalism from art—the era of unintelligibility, balance of forms, distortion of nature and ignorance of contemporary reality was over. And any inspiration from ancient times was dismissed as a speculative escape into mysticism.

Imro closed his eyes and recollected the Rubens painting of the lovesick Pan and Syrinx, the most beautiful nymph of all, who was terrified of the wild man-beast of the forest. His passion made him pursue her and he had almost caught her when she threw herself into the river where her father, the river god, instantly turned her into water reeds. So instead of embracing a naked female body, Pan had only those in his arms. He then sat on the riverbank, a breeze blowing, and heard a wistful tune coming from the reeds. Suddenly he also wanted to play music and conquer his passion that way. So he broke off some reeds of different length, joined them together with wax and blew into them to make such beautiful music that they named his pipes Syrinx.

Thus did Eliška Beňadiková tell Imro the tale of Pan when he went to her for music lessons. After the war, she and her husband had become impoverished and had to make money somehow.

The image of the small, frail figure, alone by the window with a cascade of orange leaves, etched itself into Imro's memory. He took out his sketchbook and started to draw.

Let's drink to the good old world, the one which for some reason, poor management or what, has now died on us like a mangy
old dog. Here's to its nobility which will never be resurrected, to
the operas and balls in the Budapest Vigadó and in Vienna. To car-
nival—the streets here used to be buzzing with it! To boating on
the river in summer. To the tennis tournaments in the gardens of
our manor house. To the summer nights when we would burn charcoal in the metal hog in the garden to keep us warm. There was a
door on its side for that purpose and we would scatter hay, put
down sheepskins and blankets down, drink wine, have philosoph-
ical discussions, talk about art, opera, spas in foreign parts. And
we'd canoodle, of course, and laugh ... We used to laugh so much!
Some of us even slept till morning in that fragrant hay.

As Beňadik reminisced, a twinkle came to his sunken eyes. He
turned to his wife:

Can't you play him something Lutheran?! Let Imriško see how
Lutherans prepare for Christmas. And he began singing:

'*Hort der En-gel- hel-le Lie-der, klin-gen weit*

Das Feld entlang.'

His wife's soft voice joined in with the chorus and then they
sang joyously together, Imro sipping his hot toddy and deciding
that that evening he really was in the power of insidious foxes,
ancient and Chinese. A dead girl, her things strewn about her, the
title of a song ... And what of that alleged Polish-German spy at
the manse!?

'*Glo——ri-a in ex-cel-sis De-o.*
Und die Ber-ge- hs-len wi-der von des
Hommels Lob-ge-sang.
Glo——ri-a in ex-cel-sis De-o.'

Meanwhile/fragment/, 1955

FAREWELL CLUB.

Imro, Zolo, jazz.

Somewhere, everywhere, clocks were striking eight as Imro sat up
on the metal bed of his dormitory room. He then sleepily got to
his feet, threw a towel over his shoulder and took his soap, tooth-
brush and near-empty tube of Thymolin toothpaste from the shelf.
He had to walk down a long corridor to wash in the common
washroom. The dormitory was almost empty; only a few Chinese
students were still there as well as a few locals after their graduation
ceremonies. Noises resounded down the empty space. He wanted
to go into town, to the Mánes building, the Municipal House or
the Clementinum. There might be some famous musician playing,
Oistrakh, for example, rehearsing a concerto with the orchestra.
He could stay and listen for a while; the cleaners would let him.

He would then meet with Zolo and they would go to the music
club before boarding the night-train home for the last time, now
that their studies were finally over. Imro would go to his parents'
villa while Zolo would go to Bratislava and find digs for himself
and Želka, as well as a little studio where he would paint undis-
turbed. Želka would enjoy cooking while she waited for him; in
the evening, there would be the cinema and artists' cafés. Her days
at the haberdashers were over. Two battered suitcases were packed.

Imro turned on the radio. For a moment there were just faint crackling sounds and then music. Soon, however, it was interrupted by the sonorous tones of the announcer:

'Ethel and Julius Rosenberg are dead!'

The voice continued:

'Julius died first. He had entered the room with a blank expression on his face, received three jolts of electric current and then was pronounced dead. Ethel Rosenberg followed. She hugged and kissed her guard before sitting in the chair.'

Imro stood by the window and listened to the tinny voice on the radio:

'After the first jolt, smoke could be seen coming from the leather mask Ethel was wearing on her head. Two further jolts followed and then two more . . . . In Washington, Emanuel Bloch, the Rosenbergs' legal representative, opened the door of his hotel room and allegedly said to the waiting newspapermen: "Listen and never forget!"'

And the powerful voice went silent.

The July sun shimmered above the huge square yard behind the dormitory with its courts for volleyball and basketball. Two ping-pong tables stood on the grass.

On three sides of the courtyard stood the huge wings of the functionalist school and dormitory built for the Russian aristocracy and White Guard fleeing the homeland soon after the outbreak of the revolution. On 7 November 1917, the Aurora protected cruiser was anchored in the Neva, and, at Lenin's command, fired a blank shot into the glass of the Winter Palace, shrouded that day in deep fog. It was a signal to the artillery that the assault had started.

But on that July day, in Prague near Pankrác, it was silent except for the soft rustling of the densely planted lime trees which grew along the perimeter of what they now called the Soviet school.

Imro lit a cigarette and drank cold tea from a half-litre mug—during the holidays, there was no breakfast or dinner served in the canteen. Words and fragments of sentences from recently published letters of the married couple were fluttering through his mind. Every day there were newspaper articles about opposition to the Rosenbergs' execution from all around the world. Louis Aragon's words kept coming back to him: 'If innocent blood flows, you will stain your star-spangled banner . . . If the Rosenbergs are executed, it will be a murder of innocent people . . .'

Imro recalled the endearments the two used while writing to each other in prison. Almost like how a man and woman whisper to each other after lovemaking in bed, their naked bodies pressed together: my dearest, my beautiful one, my darling wife, I love you with all my strength, tonight you can sleep peacefully my love, I am sure we'll have a wonderful future with our children . . .

On the wide parapet of the dormitory window, Imro started to sketch a cell, two boys from behind, and, opposite them, the hunched figure of a woman—their mother, who had just written to her husband: 'I'm sitting here in Sing-Sing and waiting for my legal murder . . . I am looking at pictures of our children . . . You, my dear, in the next cell, are destined to suffer the very same fate.'

Imro drew another cell with a man on the bunk and recalled fragments of the conversations between the condemned couple: 'I am glad you will be the first to meet our children . . . This morning I was tense and agitated but when your voice reached my cell, my tension subsided and the boys' shouts were like music to me' . . . 'I returned from my afternoon walk. The air is full of the salty smell of the sea'... 'Darling, they have upheld their verdict'... 'My darling, I send you all my heart'...

In the heat, the city was like a stupefied giant and one could see the hot air shimmering. Unusually, the tram was half-empty. The rattle and the occasional jingling when the guard pulled the bell cord gave Imro the feeling of being rocked in invisible arms. He was gazing out at the suburban cityscape when a student from his year said hello, a woman with a big buxom figure who the boys would tease:

Hey, Ľuba, you should have been a sculptor, not a painter. You could carve stone with a pen-knife!

Or they'd say to her in the school atelier:

Why don't you do the shot put?! You'd easily beat Zybinová and Dumbadze! and Ľuba, dressed in a white doctor's gown with lapels turned up waved the pointed end of her paintbrush at them as if to say she could pierce their canvases with it whenever she wanted. But she took no offence.

She sat down next to Imro and, delighted to have a listener, started talking in thunderous tones about Peking—where she had recently spent a few months. People turned to look when she yelled out in ecstasy how she had fallen in love with Chinese women:

They are like delicate little dolls, Imro! Their complexion is like yellow gladiolus petals and their hair like ravens, long, straight and thick as wire. Their teeth are like porcelain from the Sung dynasty and their eyes like coal from a Fu-Shung mine!

She had soon warmed to her theme.

I can't stop drawing them—let me show you. I use the ink and wash technique, and it captures them best of all. She untied the string of her portfolio, opened it out on her knees and showed Imro her work.

This is Liang. She was waiting for me at the airport. We drank orange juice and talked in sign language, she Chinese and me Slovak—until the translator came, he at least knew some Russian. She's an actress. They were just rehearsing Burjakovský's play about Fučík—Liang is playing Gusta! She takes size 36 shoes, 12 sizes smaller than me!

And she shrieked with laughter.

Next to her, I looked like a bear from the Tatras!

Imro saw the ink wash picture of what looked like an elf.

That old woman had stumps instead of feet. You still sometimes see deformed women like her in the street, hobbling along. When they were little girls, four of their toes were tied to the soles of their feet.

And poets have described their walk like the swaying of a willow in the wind, said Imro with a smile.

Imriško, how clever you are! And so refined! This one would suit you. Also very delicate but feisty, I tell you. Just like me!

She showed him another ink wash painting.

This is Buj-Li—the doctor who saved me from sunstroke on the Square of Heavenly Peace.

Ľuba described a huge ceremony with Mao in the distance in a grey-green uniform, the deafening applause, the military march, the bouquets everywhere, the doves flying, little pieces of cloth with writing on them tied to their legs, the fireworks . . . the sun was lethal, though.

And she ran her finger over her portrait of the Chinese doctor.

Buj-Li had plaits and looked about twenty-five but then she introduced me to her fourteen-year-old daughter. Not for you, I'm afraid. Nor this determined woman—Ting-Ling is her name and she looked like a peasant . . . I did those gnarled hands pretty well, don't you think?! A simple coat and jacket but she's actually a writer and wants to live the real life of a working peasant woman! I guess that actress from the airport who played Gusta would suit you the best. You could rock her on your knee and she'd stroke your head and sad face, Imro, Imríček.

Ľuba stroked Imro and kissed him on the cheek.

Does she really speak Russian? I'm still learning the language.

Imro laughed more than he had in a long time. The tram lurched from side to side and he enjoyed looking at the solid shapes of his classmate's ink wash paintings. Only her efforts at new themes and a new ideology were rendered in an old-fashioned manner, and Imro knew that he wanted to go in another direction. He wanted to depict introspective figures, curled up like fetuses, pictures which were individualistic and not collective, pictures which were open to interpretation. He hated those outstretched figures on all the posters in the streets, looking as if they had a string inside elongating them and giving to their faces a perpetual false cheeriness. Or exhibitions of still lifes with *Pravda* on the table, pictures of combines and tractors, flowers in vases and Stalin's writings in the background. Everything was so crude, wooden and artificial! Even though as students they all had to leave school for a week or two to spend time in a factory or collective farm, their work lacked spark. Every new era in history called for some new artistic protest or anarchy. It was important to see things in a new way, and not through the lens of the stiff academicism with which most of their teachers had struggled.

Ľuba noisily continued:

And here I have one quick sketch from the Chinese opera.

Two actors sat on floor cushions on the stage while a third stood behind a drum. Above their heads Ľuba had written what was apparently the name of the opera: *Third Attack on the Village of Tzu Chvang Tio.*

I really liked the parts on the two-string balalaika and the wooden drum sounded nice, but then they hit the large and small gong and the sound boards and I almost ran off. And then suddenly it was all quiet, and, just imagine, the actors had a smoke on stage and then went on with the show. Here is one from my work brigade here . . . In the factory, the women still couldn't get used to wearing overalls. This old dear from the sticks was happily standing by the machine in her folk costume, even wearing an apron her daughter-in-law had sewn for her. You've got to show off what you've got, you see! Only when she was leaning over, a thread got caught in the machine and the whole lot came undone together with all her skirts! Don't look at me—I wasn't there, I just heard about it! What a chump she was! The foreman must have had hell to pay.

Ľuba turned over the last of her drawings and tied the string of her portfolio.

What a glorious day, Imrík—a perfect day for boating, for pulling oars through the water and watching how beautifully our muscles work. A person is a beautiful machine to ensure a beautiful future for all collective-minded people. Whereas you, my sad clown, are an embodiment of the tragedy of individualism.

And as she declaimed, she pulled his head close to hers.

You sound like something from a pamphlet, Ľuba. Straight off one of the posters!

But the girl wasn't offended and they both laughed, though Imro's laughter was rather forced. And then Ľuba got off—she had a meeting with their tutor to show her her new drawings from China. He was going a few more stops.

He watched the everyday theatre—in the tram, at the stops, in the streets and on the pavements—men, women, children. There were perhaps fewer than usual today, walking quietly as though mute, quickly, not noticing one another. The hottest time of day was approaching and the air was cracking. Or at least that's how it seemed to Imro.

He purged such moments of their joy because he had learnt to look at everything through a lens of doubt and skepticism, as if through a second skin.

He got off, walked along a busier street and saw a film magazine for sale in a newsstand. He liked films and sometimes drew scenes from them, immersing himself completely into their parallel world. When he opened the magazine, he recognized the face of a German actress he had seen in a few films; she usually played a femme fatale or a dangerous foreigner. He started to read: 'Sybille Schmitz, who filmgoers from the 1930s and 40s will certainly remember, struggled with alcohol and various harmful drugs before taking her life in mysterious circumstances a few months ago. At the time, she was being cared for by a lesbian doctor with whom she allegedly lived and who may have given her an overdose of morphine. The actress' relatives are threatening the doctor with legal action . . . Sybille became famous at a very young age, though she was not to Hitler's taste—her features being more Semitic than Aryan. She even had contacts with the Jewish community, which meant that Nazi ideologues quietly urged filmmakers not to cast her. After the war, she was forced to adopt a new look and play more optimistic roles . . . .' The article closed with the statement: 'This talented actress could not cope with not being able to use her undoubted talent in the immoral world of the West German film industry.'

Old shadows lurking, thought Imro.

He sat down by the Vltava for a while, munching on a pretzel and narrowing his eyes to avoid the glare of the sun on the water. He was very warm in the black corduroy jacket he had first worn at his graduation and decided to wear ever since as an individual outfit of protest against all the blind optimists out there. He browsed through the magazine and came across some photos from a documentary film, *From the Haunted City*.

Some people had faces, half of which had turned grey; bodies, face down, were floating in canals. Corpses hung amid the ruins of houses while children, their eyes open, slept in school classrooms. An insane woman was pressing her breast to her dead child; another had severe burns on her face . . . . There was then a sardonic text saying that first-rate plastic surgeons were inviting Hiroshima women with badly scarred faces to America so that with their scalpels they could restore them to their old beauty. Imro read the article alongside:

'Some saboteur could very easily drop atomic dust in our streets and the living would die.'

Imro stopped nibbling on the pretzel and broke it up for the birds on the Vltava. Its sour aftertaste was not improved by the picture of a young worker, with perfect teeth and hair, his shirt and overalls all streaked with diesel. Alongside his broad Socialist smile was the slogan: 'Diesel doesn't stink to a model worker but is as fragrant as perfume'. Beneath the photo was the punchline printed in large letters: 'Because diesel belongs to everyone'.

He put the magazine in his pocket. He would go first to the pharmacy to say goodbye to Špitz's brother and his wife, would drink a quick cup of coffee with them in the room behind the shop where they mixed various oils, powders and drops and where there was a smell of something soporific like sleeping gas.

Then he would go to see Zolo in his dormitory. It was always fun there perhaps because the building had once been a brothel entered via an old gateway.

Zolo shared a room with five others in which there were three metal bunkbeds, three cupboards and three tables. Through the window you could see only a church tower and the sky. At the end of the week, the manager of the dormitory would sometimes come to Zolo's room because they were 'future artists, sensitive souls' living there and he would read to them extracts from the detective stories and sentimental novels he wrote in the evenings but which no one wanted to publish.

What should I read you today, boys? An extract from *Nella's Innocent Prostitutes* or one from *The Pussycats and the Diamond*?

Something with murders in it, Comrade Manager! yelled Zolo and the manager read in an affectedly deep voice the story of a murder involving a former servant, Nelinka, who was with child and thus disowned by her parents and fired from the estate where she worked. She found herself on the street, gave birth and her child was taken from her and put in an orphanage. She then ended up in this former—*fortunately* (and he emphasized the word) former—house of ill repute (he never called it a brothel), where she was murdered by a jealous client. Her poor orphan later became a tramp on the street. But whether it had all really happened, the comrade director was not willing to say.

That's one of art's secrets, boys! An eternal secret! And he spoke with his finger raised portentously.

At other times, his wife would read to the boys 'something by Mrs Boženka' or by 'our Mrs Eliška' and the boys listened merrily as she clucked one of her favourite passages: 'so this is the *talent*, Hálek said to Rigr and looked at me with obvious surprise. In the Rigrs' salon, I was attended to by the noble, charming and famous Jan Evangelista Purkyně. He was a dear old man and delightful companion—oh how I detested the dancer who dragged me away from him . . . but I only want to speak about the people who accompanied me to the Czech Parnassus . . .'

Finally leaving their dormitories, Imro and Zolo agreed to go to the music club for the last time; they'd get a taxi to take their suitcases to the station. They'd pool their funds somehow for it—they were both broke after their recent graduation celebrations.

The club was a small room, half-underground, with a little stage for musicians, tables with old armchairs and a tiny bar. Because the only light came from a few windows beneath the ceiling, there were candles in wine bottles burning on the bar. The glass of the bottles was almost invisible so coated were they by tears of wax.

When the two entered, their friend Džano was sticking posters on the wall of a jazz club in New York. On the opposite side were repros of pictures Imro had brought—all by painters of the *Neue Sachlichkeit*: a scene from Metropolis by Otto Dix, a satirical portrait from Grosz's *Gott mit uns* cycle and a copy of his *Eclipse of the Sun* as well as a *Party in Paris* by Max Beckmann. Their new, matter-of-fact objectivity gave a picture of the deformed world of Germany between the wars; Imro felt with every pore the sense of collective madness in them which was soon to break out in Fascist Germany and traumatize the world together with the microworld of every single person, he and his family included. In the boldly coloured and expressively stylized scenes which Hitler described as Degenerate Art, the musicians on the canvases were often playing jazz—a genre which the Fuhrer also condemned as degenerate.

You see, Imro! And we're of the generation that can go no further than Prague!

And Zolo pointed to the reproductions as he stretched out in his armchair with a beer in his hand. Džano put a record on the gramophone—live music started at seven. The sounds of Django Reinhardt's 'Les Yeux Noirs' filled the room and Džano joined his friends with a beer.

That, Zolo, is what we need to change! We need to get out and see the world, like the aristos in the old days. To stand in front of the Masters face to face, in front of their canvases and frescos in all their immensity. To look at the modern masterpieces of the West, not our stifling one-dimensional versions of them. We are responsible for creating new forms. If the old world is really finishing, we have to be courageous and tell the truth.

Imriško the Silent finally finds his tongue—how good to listen to you! Do take me with you on your travels. Oh, to drink absinthe or whisky, something famous that isn't ours, in one of the New York clubs and listen to the jazz geniuses till the sun comes up! In fact till death, because I don't think I could live without it or without you! When are you coming back!? Prague's the place to be—never forget it!

Džano occasionally got up to change the record. The three drank beer, listened and took deep drags on their cigarettes. Imro and Zolo were silent as Džano expounded his theme to the rhythm of the music:

Jazz, jazz, that's what lifts me up another level. Jazz and alcohol but jazz is better because there is no price to pay afterwards—and a few nice girls in bed. That's what's missing here—some naked girls on the walls—it's like in a monastery. I'm doing all kinds of stuff these days, even taxi driving, but I'd rather play—but not for snobs or posers. I'd like to have a real jazz world—spiritual. My own band, a sax that sounds like velvet, to play jazz sessions, music with a new idea and new vitality in this sinking world of ours, music to make all the cant and crap, all the claptrap around us just evaporate and leave us to play as freely as an animal in the savannah. And to always have that strength, that freedom! It's not playing foxtrots in some collective brain-numbing drill but listening to the pianist, to how he's clearing space for you to come in and do your thing, whatever that might be. You are not a trainee playing according to some rubric, like some pussycat with soft claws. Yes, you might want to caress your audience but you also want to let them know you're playing not because someone has told you to—but because you want to blow out all your soul, all your melancholy and joy. Have another beer and a rum chaser, it is our last evening in our little jazz shell, my friends. I shan't be seeing you off at the station.

And he spoke without taking a breath.

The small room gradually started to fill up with students, a few soldiers appeared and then the other musicians Džano was going to play with. One carried a beer to the drums, another was testing the microphone, the pianist ran his fingers along the keys and played a few chords. Džano stood on the stage, his saxophone in his mouth and blared out a high note. Then when the melody started to ascend like a snake, his solo soared up above it melting into the surrounding air.

Imro and Zolo lay on their couchettes in the train compartment, both on their back, their left hands behind their head, cigarettes in their right. They left the little night light switched on, saying nothing as they reflected on the end of an era. And then Imro spoke:

Zolo, it is funny but I've got this feeling that we may be the last generation to take everything so damn seriously!

They laughed and coughed as they smoked.

And who will just be sitting around marking time. Nothing is going to happen. It's all stagnating!

There is always something happening.

Zolo wanted to protest but Imro continued.

But now we're all being forced to conform. Nothing and no one can stand out.

The houses and lamp-posts of the suburbs raced past, with the moon above to one side . . .

Look Imro, there is your moon—this time made from grey-green satin and quite different from your strontium moons and suns!

Imro reminded Zolo how their neurotic chemistry teacher, always with a cane in his head, tested them on the periodic table. Once when the boys couldn't stop laughing, he caned their backs so hard that Imro's eyes had stung. Just as when he caught them looking at Zolo's erotic pictures of Želka under the desk.

Imro used to like chemistry, and, after Hiroshima and Nagasaki, had again started to read books about it—even though it had been responsible for those two atrocities.

The symbol of strontium is Sr and atomic number 38. Strontium-90 is a radioactive isotope which occurs in fallout from nuclear bombs and accidents with a half-life of 28.8 years.

Imro repeated the words in his head as if revising for a test.

But their time in the rattling train was peaceful. Leaving the past behind, they moved closer to what was awaiting them. Imro was silent for a while and then responded:

Yeah, my moons are always yellowish—like strontium—or grey and black. I will have to add this bottlegreen variety, Zolík, you're right!

We've been through a lot in Prague, Imriško! Do you think we will ever forget about it?

I've learnt not to forget what I've seen. Otherwise everything will keep coming back like when the wind whirls around your head. And something has changed in us—in the structure of our brain and heart, my friend.

So thought Imro but he didn't give utterance to such thoughts. Zolo would have mocked him for his pathos.

Meanwhile/fragment/, 1959–1960

THE SAD CLOWN AND THE NEWBORN.

Imro, Emilka and Sára.

After his return from Prague, Imro's relationship with his father was not like before. The hunched old man felt it too, shuffling from room to room, occasionally watering the few surviving plants and flowers in the conservatory. Perhaps their survival was also due to the former gardener coming to look after them, a sign of the good memories he had of the villa and its residents. Only his visits were getting fewer and fewer—apparently he had started coughing up blood.

Štern sent good coffee to his former friend via Imro and old employees of what had been Gallo's meat and sausage concern (now state-owned), sent them fatty poultry pastes and klobasa because no one in town provided kosher products anymore.

Imro was soon going every morning to the library, where he could forget the image of his grey and emaciated father spending whole days sitting in bed, rocking to and fro and moving his lips. Sometimes he would mutter the name of his wife and sigh:

Oh, what a disaster it all is!

And he'd read in a soft voice from the Book of Job, even though, in the past, he had never been one for spiritual matters. Imro would hear odd fragments:

'. . . which doeth great things and unsearchable; marvellous things without number! . . . to set up on high those that be low; that those which mourn may be exalted to safety.'

Imro brought him lime-blossom tea with honey but his father wouldn't drink it. He went on muttering:

'Therefore despise not thou the chastening of the Almighty: For he maketh sore, and bindeth up: he woundeth, and his hands make whole. He shall deliver thee in six troubles: yea, in seven there shall no evil touch thee.'

Then one morning, his father didn't sit up in bed when Imro brought him his chosen breakfast of a roll sliced up and soaked in hot milk. He looked like Imro's mother had once looked, as if asleep in the vacuum of a never-ending night.

Afterwards Emilka always got the daily newspapers and art magazines ready for Imro's visits to the library. He looked forward to going, to seeing the helpful, fair-haired new librarian. Her skin smelled of something pleasant he could not identify. Her eyes were child-like, hinting at naivety and the willingness to give her all to others. Yes, her blue eyes were naive! Imro told her she had eyes of dew:

The eyes of a dew-covered rosebud, such is the look you give me. You should have been called Rose.

Emilka smiled—she was flattered. None of the other boys had said anything like that to her. Imro liked her callow enthusiasm, her undisguised enjoyment of life. And in no way did she remind Imro of the little girl from the transport. She was not ashamed of her laughter, of unexpected happiness, of her own sexuality.

Only Imro suddenly felt lost at home—the place was empty without either of his parents there. Shadows crept along the floors, and there was damp on the walls from the house not being properly aired. Because of the excessive size of the living space, tenants were moved in even while his father was still alive but they often quarrelled.

When Imro fell ill, it took a long time for doctors to make a diagnosis and no one knew what course the illness would take. There was a lack of medicine and no one gave him much hope. He kept going for blood tests to a new building with a hammer and sickle above the entrance and a sign reading: 'District Institute of National Health'.

At the start of summer, his doctor suggested he have his first exhibition there. His oil paintings, gouaches and pencil drawings were soon hanging in the long corridors where evenly spaced marble columns held up the ceiling. There were pictures of young townswomen, their figures or profiles, large sad heads of clowns and ladies on horseback, a pale girl, a man in bloodied clothes with a parrot, refugees from somewhere, landscapes with bowing willow branches, solitary trees, towns with a low-lying moon hovering above a river, all covered with thick black strokes which made the shapes almost invisible. After the exhibition, local officials realized that the town now had its own artist—a painter who needed a large studio. The tenants who had been forced to move into the villa were summarily moved out.

Things started to change after Emilka moved into the house. It was a very small wedding; at Imro's insistence, only Zolo and Želka were invited. Emilka was small but full of energy, as dynamic as the monkey on elastic she once won at a fairground rifle range because Imro did not want to hold a gun in his hand. By the stall where you could win paper roses, monkeys and teddy bears, he told her how in Prague—during his military service lessons he was sent out to march with a local student of acting, a practical joker and at the same time a fearless rebel:

Are you Imro? I'm Jan. Listen, let's pretend we have forgotten all the commands.

When the sergeant bellowed at them:

Stop. About turn!

The new boys carried on marching until another one was sent to call them back. Later they explained to the investigatory committee that they had forgotten all other commands.

The adjutant roared at them:

You artists and actors, you're just a bunch of insolent good-for-nothings. Get out of my sight!

Emilka laughed and bounced the monkey up and down.

Your laughter is like pearls, like balsam to my sickened soul.

Imro kissed Emilka on her mouth among the crowds of people milling between the rides and the stalls. She claimed that the homemade kefir she had learned to make would cure him of his mysterious endless fatigue; on the sideboard in the kitchen, there were always jars of milk with special cultures added. She took pleasure in the first crocuses, tulips and daffodils in the newly cleared garden, in the aroma and cleanness of the house which her father—secretary of the party's district committee—very quickly had redecorated and done up for them. A child was on its way.

The groundfloor rooms served as atelier and storeroom for Imro and his paintings. Emilka did not like going there. She felt like an intruder; all those cryptic pictures hanging up or leaning against the wall troubled the beautiful head of the young librarian. Instead, she set about cleaning up the conservatory, throwing out some of the dead palms and oleander and having new plants brought in from the botanical garden in the county town. She collected little lime trees from her aquaintances, growing out of fashion in front of their living-room windows, as well as China roses, some of which were just blossoming with waxy burgundy petals. She planted lots of cacti and succulents, and went among the plants on hands and knees though her swollen belly was making it awkward for her. And she didn't notice it when Imro remained hidden in his studio even when she came home from work. She devoted immense reserves of energy to the conservatory, so that nothing dark and unpleasant would ever claim the epicentre of her mind.

Imro had a bed moved to the studio so that he could lie down when his fatigue became unbearable. He complained of his arms and legs tingling and of losing strength. Often, he would get a chill and then a fever soon afterwards. He refused food and sweated so profusely that Emilka had to change his bedding in the middle of the night.

As well as painting, he wrote a lot. He wanted to open a theatre of light or vision in the town and often experimented with light and shade in the studio. One evening he called Emilka to play a game of cat's cradle with him in which they looped colourful cotton thread around their fingers to create various strange patterns. He then shone a light on their hands and the moving geometrical images were projected onto the wall. He put some soft music on the gramophone and asked Emilka if she felt inner peace. Embarrassed, she nodded to make him happy. He then played a recording of glass shattering and asked her if it gave her a sense of danger.

He projected a broken window and a man with a screwed-on loud-speaker on his shoulders instead of a head. He spoke fervently to Emilka about how he would write a play dealing with the eternal struggle between good and evil; the actors would be chess pieces, the black-and-white board would be huge, infinite and a troubled human soul would hang over it. He superimposed poems on to a moon projected on the wall, either on to that recurrent greenish moon of his or on to one which was light grey.

Emilka was breathless when she arrived home. It was the height of summer and she had one more week's work to do before going on maternity leave. She took off her little red wide-brimmed hat and the beige summer jacket she wore to stop her back and shoulders getting sunburnt (her dress, made of the same material as the jacket, was sleeveless and had a deep square neck). She was just removing her red shoes when she heard a gentle piping sound. She smiled. He must be in a good mood if he was playing his flute; occasionally, he still also played the violin and piano. Perhaps that long stay in the Prague clinic which Štern's brother arranged really had helped him. She walked barefoot to the atelier door and opened it very quietly.

Next to her stood a clown in a long black cape made of stain. His face, lit up against the black wall behind, was a floury white; his mouth was a red smirk and Emilka was angry when she realized Imro had used her lipstick to do it. Black painted tears trickled down his face, halfway up his forehead he had painted on black eyebrows and taking funny little steps in his white socks, he set the self timer to take photos of himself in various poses.

Imro! she yelled twice and then crouched down next to the door.

What have you done to yourself, for heaven's sake? I'm afraid of you, Imriško! Wash it all off!

Imro crouched down next to her:

Emilka. I'm playing the part of a clown whose sadness was so great that it outgrew even love.

But his poetic pathos upset her even more and she started to sob noisily like a child. Her large belly shook heavily—it was uncomfortable for her but the birth was still a few months away.

Imro kissed her hair and wiped her tears away with it.

Oh my darling, my dearest, don't take it to heart! I should have told you . . . But you know how obsessed I am, how I'm always looking for new artistic forms, how a brush and paints are not enough for me. This is how I play! Aren't you glad that I'm playing, that I don't have a chill, that they gave me some hope in Prague? Medicine is advancing all the time, the professor is an expert in those stupid glands and their tumours. And he's a friend of the late Mr Štern's brother, the pharmacist! I'm not so tired today—you don't have to tie the brush to my wrist if I want to paint.

Imro, please, take off that horrible mask—it's not in the least bit funny! You are like a ghost. It is all so dark! So . . . sinister! Black satin, white socks. Your hair all vaselined—what have you done? And the way you tiptoe around . . . ! It's as if you're from another world, communing with ghosts. You shouldn't be doing it. You mustn't! I'm afraid of you . . . Anyway, I'm going upstairs. Come up afterwards . . . !

And Emilka went on whimpering, little knowing that she had taken on some of his nightmares and that he, unwittingly, had passed them on to her.

After Sára's birth, Emilka's nipples were often very sore. She put silver nitrate on them which the doctor had given her in a little bottle when she last took Sára to be checked and weighed. The baby girl slept hard still pressed to the breast. Emilka softly sang the words of a lullaby she had read in the library and for which she invented her own melody:

'Sleep, little baby, lie there in clover. Lie there till morning, today's games are over.'

And she tenderly ran her fingertips through the newborn's dark hair.

I have a granddaughter like a bilberry! Welcome! cooed Emilka's father when he saw her for the first time. And then he said with a chuckle:

She is the first dark girl in our family.

Emilka's mother joined in:

She's just like her father, that little one!

Imro did not care much for meeting Emilka's parents but she did not blame him for it as she could see he was getting weaker. His chills and bouts of sweating alternated with greater frequency and he got so weak, he could neither stand nor sit; he lay in the unmade bed where Emilka breastfed the baby and played with her. Imro liked the heat his wife created—her side of the bed was always warmer than his. He loved the delicate smell which she left on her pillow and even the sour odour of his daughter's vomit was not unpleasant.

He somehow joined himself to her little body drawing strength and energy from it. She was like a refreshing breeze for him. Only he had little to say to Emilka's father. His job as secretary of the party's district branch repelled him—he did not want to know anything about it and felt guilty by association. He didn't want any help from his father-in-law even though he refurbished the house himself while Imro lay for a long time in a Prague hospital.

We are not made of the same stuff, you and me! I just want to help the old proletariat which I was once a member of. I don't want to harm anybody. We just call things by different names.

His father-in-law tried to bridge the gap between them—he could feel Imro's aversion.

When things are called by the wrong names, then lies build up!

But Imro's words only irritated him and the two avoided each other, even as Imro's condition got worse.

He is not one of us—he's different, whether he wants it or not. Emilka has no life with him. Even his weird illness—let's be honest about it—there is no cure, is there?

Be quiet! Don't speak like that! You should never give up hope!

And his wife, a secret Catholic, protested angrily but then softened her voice to propitiate her husband:

His mother always stood out. His father was more approachable if I remember rightly but she was proud and held her head up high. A strong woman, no doubt! She was in the Red Cross. One time, just before they evacuated to the village, she helped care for the wounded and even worked in the hospital laundry—the other ladies in town would have recoiled at the thought. And then she ran away from the Germans . . . And then she died, no one knew how. She wanted to set up a healthcare school here.

I know—I've got nothing against the Jews—they've been through a lot. But I just can't hit it off with that son-in-law of ours and shan't be seeking his company. If he looks down on me, so be it. It's his choice, not mine.

After Imro came back from the clinic in Prague, his mother-in-law was again happy to cook him the ham bakes, venison risotto, little tarts, fruit juices and blancmange he could just about manage as his swallowing got worse. She would sit on the side of his bed and when he fell asleep in exhaustion, would take out her rosary beads and pray quietly for him.

He wanted to be alone and could not put up with anyone anymore, only Emilka and the baby girl. He thought:

Sára is like humanity reborn. The first innocent person.

The growing child started to copy the form of his face, especially his eyes. He spoke to her of weighty matters and she would gaze wide-eyed at him without blinking. One day she suddenly released from her throat a whole orchestra of sounds. She then went silent, waited for her father's voice and again issued a throaty call.

So I have had my first conversation with my daughter, he said and laughed tenderly.

Sometimes the baby girl grabbed his cheeks with her fingers or bumped her mouth against his chin. He watched as she started to form words, to apprehend the world around her and instantly try to comment on it. He once bought three clockwork metal hens, wound them up and let them go tottering on the floor and pecking at it as the three people crawled after them, laughing. Sára squealed, banged her fists on the ground, and, when one of the hens stopped, she wanted to stamp on it in the new shoes which her mother had bought her. He swung Sára in his arms, lifted her up high; she shrieked with joy and her laughter was an antidote. He taught her to draw circles and smaller circles inside larger ones; she preferred the unbroken movement of drawing them to the stop-start task of drawing triangles, squares and rectangles. Little Sára liked circles best of all.

Again it seemed that Imro's health was improving, that this new being was energizing him. And again he started to experiment with photo collage, setting the auto timer on his Flexaret and taking photos of himself with different facemasks he painted on. He then developed the photos, dried them and cut them into little pieces. But Emilka did not go into the studio. She guessed that Imro had gone back to his old experiments and had no wish to see them.

He started playing his musical instruments again—the piano, violin and flute, their sounds filling the house like in the old days. He would play his mother's favourite song on the violin: 'Tum-bala, tum-bala, tum-balalaika . . .' Emilka took Sára in her arms and danced with her, singing the catchy melody with her husband. During the sharp turns, Sára would laugh with a strong throaty voice that amazed them.

But then the illness came back with its old intensity and Imro again asked Emilka to tie the brush to his wrist. Painting that way was less strenuous and he managed to finish a picture in grey-green. It was of a naked prophet, agitated and gesticulating, his arms raised up and his fists clenched, a prophet whose words his father had once read:

'But a man dies and is laid low;
he breathes his last and is no more.
As the water of a lake dries up
or a riverbed becomes parched and dry,
so he lies down and does not rise;
till the heavens are no more, people will not awake
or be roused from their sleep.'

Imro knew that he was breaking free. During the last months, when the skin hung off his bones and he looked liked the hunched figure in that last painting, just he and Emilka were there in the

house. She would smile bravely, play him records on the gramophone, read out passages from books he chose. Of the records, there
was one Polish chanson he wanted to listen to—'*Ciemna dziś noc
...*' Afterwards he wept, said that he was guilty because there had
been a crime he hadn't reported and now he was paying for it.
Emilka did not understand him at all and thought it was his
fever making him delirious. Then the record disappeared—he didn't
want to listen to it anymore and was suddenly cheerful again. His
strength returned and he only wanted to listen to jazz.

Play me this one from heaven. He probably went there will-
ingly.

So that afternoon Emilka took Charlie Parker's 'All the Things
You Are' out of its paper sleeve.

Imro got up and took her ever-soft, acquiescent form in his
arm. She was as malleable and light as the saxophone playing and
he tried to dance, Emilka pressing her face to his shoulder so that
she would see nothing, neither his face, nor the gramophone on
the bedside locker, nor the window open to the garden where the
autumn asters had just started to blossom, nor the gazebo where
they sometimes went to get some fresh air. She didn't want to see
anything.

After the dance, Imro slowly went down to the studio below,
took out his sketchpad and drew a dancing pair, locked together,
in charcoal. He then made quick strokes to blur and obscure the
dancing figures and create two separate layers of blackness.

When the housekeeping money in the drawer ran out, Emilka
secretly took some of his drawings and smaller pictures of those
towns levitating at night or of figures covered by black smears and
offered them to colleagues at the library. They were usually struck

by the melancholy and strange stylization of the figures, so far removed from reality; occasionally, someone bought something. And then one day one of them said:

When your husband dies, will his pictures be more expensive?

Emilka felt she had been punched in the head. It was like something she had recently seen on television—two heavyweight boxers murderously thrashing it out until one of them lay unconscious on the ground and the referee counted him out. From then on Emilka never offered his pictures to her colleagues. She would go to the market for something, hold the frame in front of her like an icon and ask passing strangers if they wanted to buy a picture for their living room.

Sára stayed with her grandparents during this time; Imro didn't want his wasted body to be her abiding image of him. Imro visualized her face and how she moved her little protruding tongue between her lips when she drew those endless circles of hers. He was glad that she had chosen circles and remembered the words of the old philosopher who said that in a circle the beginning and the end are the same. In a circle, one point is equal to all the other points—the circle is a symbol of equality. Whereas the triangle, with its apex, symbolizes power and subordination.

Sára is like humanity reborn. The first innocent person.

He kept repeating it over and over, recalling with a smile the pale blue body she had once had when she stretched out her arms and legs on the kitchen table after having a bath. Lying on her back like that, she reminded him of a frog or some other animal into which the pure soul of his daughter had entered.

Meanwhile/fragment/, 1968

LOVE WITH A REVOLUTIONARY.

Iboja and Giorgio.

The two of them first met in the museum when the woman guarding the exhibits sent Giorgio to speak to the young new historian. He had been asking for information about the history of the museum and the town—and he wanted it in English.

When Giorgio came in, Iboja was looking out through the bars on the small window of the old manor—the only one which had survived at what was once known as the 'top of town'. Now it was a museum. The young woman glanced at the dark-haired newcomer as if he were a vision—he himself was startled by her look as he later told her. She saw before her a man who was the very image of her grandfather in one of the photos from his youth. He had the same big, dark eyes, curly hair of a dark rust colour, gingery goatee and snub, upturned nose. Only her grandfather was never as tall or as slim as this foreigner who was saying something in English about how he wanted to get to know the culture of the town and be present during the social revolution going on, one which had surprised the West with its very real vision of a more humane society, of socialism with a human face; and how he, a Maoist, was thinking very hard about it all because the old world was rotting away and needed new projects by social architects—

even the Chinese Cultural Revolution was showing its cracks. He talked about the student unrest around the world and continued in his impassioned monologue when they were sitting together in a nearby café.

Iboja drank Viennese coffee while he drank Georgian cognac. She was happy just to listen to this garrulous Italian—her English was not very good and she was not used to speaking freely on such topics. She had been sitting for a few months in a new dreamlike world of almost no people, among stuffed animals and birds, old aristocratic and peasant costumes, fine porcelain, prehistoric stones and bones in showcases. Now this fiery young man was pulling her out of her shell and ordering a cognac for her (she did not even protest). They then walked round the town and with sudden pleasure she was telling him which wealthy Jews and Christians had lived in which houses, describing the wide range of industries and trades which had been gradually aryanized during the war. And if any of the Jews had returned from the deathcamps, she told him, their property was soon nationalized. Now in the lower floors of the buildings there were still shops but their choice of goods was limited; upstairs, there lived gipsies because their settlements had been liquidated and the new powers-that-be wanted these remnants from the dawn of civilization to be equal to the whites. Or there were offices or other public services upstairs.

She showed him both churches: the Catholic church on the square and the Lutheran one slightly to the side. Beyond the houses at the upper end of town, Giorgio was surprised to see a large, artfully concealed synagogue.

I belong to them, she said bluntly, and promised that the next day he could go inside. She would go to the secretary of the Jewish community, which had only ten members and who met in the synagogue's antechamber. It was there that they prayed and washed;

in the huge interior, books from the former yeshiva were piled up on the pews. Soon they would be taken abroad—it had long been arranged. But those few remaining Jews would go on praying in the antechamber. There was even talk of the synagogue being demolished and some of those new Finnish-style blocks of flats being built on the site.

She then sat in his small Fiat and showed him the way to a famously unspoilt village, frozen in time, with houses which looked like they had been modelled by hand. Giorgio took photos of the old people in their folk costumes. They did not object but warmly greeted the foreigner—and the two young people replied with embarrassment. The high mountains, so close at hand, were turning blue in the summer evening!

When Giorgio led Iboja to their house, he stroked her hand softly. She returned the gesture naturally and when he kissed her for the first time, she could feel his body quivering.

The next day when she went for lunch, she told her colleague she was going to the archives to study. Giorgio was waiting for her, sitting on the steps between the huge Doric columns at the front of the synagogue. Soon an old man in a shabby suit appeared, patted Iboja on the shoulder and unlocked the high doors so that Giorgio could take photos of the immense cupola, the gallery and the fading geometric wall paintings. Then they went to the Jewish cemetery, and, from there, once their guide had carefully locked the gate, to the church cemetery. As at the Jewish cemetery, Iboja showed Giorgio the graves of some of the town's most important inhabitants.

I didn't know that I was staying so close to the cemetery. And that you had so many important people here!

Giorgio smiled and pointed to the Hotel Aurora where he was staying. Iboja furrowed her brow; he noticed and asked what was wrong but she just waved a hand and picked up from the path some crepe flowers held together with wire before putting them back on the grave the wind had blown them from. They again parted in front of their house, neither of them knowing that early next morning they would wake up to the sound of trains rumbling past loaded with Soviet tanks, of armoured cars and military lorries blocking the main road through town. And in the turrets would be silent soldiers with young faces and mostly Asian features, with rifles on their shoulders. And very soon crowds of furious people would be throwing tomatoes, waving their fists and shouting at these foreign soldiers, writing messages of protest on shop windows and sticking hand-made caricatures to the fronts of houses. Giorgio and Iboja sat drawing caricatures in the café as the waiter brought them free lemonade and Turkish coffee. The town and the country were simmering. The foreign troops had stirred up a frenzy of courage and shock among the young and fear among the old.

Iboja was wearing light summer culottes and a woven vest with orange-brown stripes. She wasn't wearing a bra and her little nipples were visible. Giorgio gazed at her fascinated, and, when he could no longer resist touching her breast, she said with total naturalness:

We can't go to my place—I live with my sick grandmother. We can go to the Aurora but I can't be seen by anyone there. It used to be my grandfather's hotel and some of the staff still know me. Do you understand?!

Of course! replied Giorgio spellbound and put his arms around her. Both were now caught in the spider's web of a restless, dream-like fever.

I never guessed there was so much life in you! he later said, slipping off Iboja's body after love making, off her hot and moist skin and just away from her rapid breath.

Don't tell me that Italian women are not full of life! replied Iboja sitting up with her legs straddled across Giorgio's thighs.

Not so passionate. Our town girls are not nearly so liberated and strong as you are.

I had to learn it, what do you think!? I'd also be happy to be a princess waited on hand and foot.

I don't believe you! You're different. And don't let me out of your sight anymore!

There are other magnets!

Such as?

Revolutions! And she started laughing.

It's you! You! Only you! You're the only one in the world for me and always will be!

He pressed himself against her girlish form, her damp skin again feeling her slender bones beneath him. Then, between kisses, he began to whisper words of love in Italian to her while she did the same in Slovak, their two languages merging like their bodies.

By evening, the commotion in the square had slightly subsided but there were people everywhere. Iboja briefly spoke with acquaintances, mostly her former classmates from the *gymnázium*; everyone had gathered there, speaking rapidly and gesticulating in agitation. One boy said that a partisan war would break out and he would be joining them up in the mountains.

We can't surrender. It's an illegal occupation of a sovereign state! We'll not give in!

And he shouted and waved his fist and some people clapped him as they discussed what to do. The green snake of military cars had now slithered out of the square and beyond. Funereal classical music alternating with news of events from the larger cities came from the transistor radios a few men were carrying on their shoulders and around which pockets of people had collected.

Giorgio was talking fervently to a group of young people, telling them his theories of world revolution and the need for new 'sunshine states' if people were not to lose their dignity and be enslaved by the rich and powerful.

Camarades, camarades!

Soon they were slapping one another on their backs, their tension and fear replaced by the sudden euphoria of nothing being lost!

Let's go to the river—let's go and swim! suggested Iboja.

The unregulated wide river washed against the bank where willow trees and grass were growing. No one else was there so Iboja took off her dress and underwear, jumped in and was soon some way out. Giorgio followed her but when he realized how cold the water was, he started to shriek and hurried back to the riverbank.

It's good that I've got wet hair—at least Grandma won't ask me where I've been and who with! I've been swimming in the river and that's it! she said when they kissed goodbye in the car in front of her house.

Gosh! So much happening in just one day! So much to process!

When he had stopped howling like a wolf, Giorgio ran his fingers through his wet hair and cracked his knuckles.

And who knows what's going to happen in this country. Nothing will be the same again—we may even be separated.

Iboja kissed Giorgio as if for the last time and quickly, without looking back, ran through the gate to the tenement block where her sick grandmother would be waiting for her, doubtless alarmed by the news from the little transistor radio that lay on her belly all day. When Iboja came in, the first thing she said was:

I always said that it was a stupid system and that it would end stupidly! But I never thought it would be Big Brother who would come to crush us!

And she gave a guttural laugh.

Auntie Zuzka sat by the legs of the old woman patching up a threadbare old apron and praying in a hushed voice.

The smells of the room hardly ever changed even though it was aired every day: medicine, camphor, the oils which the masseuse applied to the immobile old woman's body a few times every week, a hint of ammonia and the scent of the carnations on the table which Giorgio had given her the day before. Now Iboja had to change her grandmother's nappy, prepare her evening and night medication and get the supper ready.

When she looked up, she saw the eager face of a chronically ill old woman turned to her—a woman with eyes still bright and keen to see everything.

You still haven't told me who the carnations are from. People don't just give bouquets out willy-nilly.

Oh, wouldn't you like to know, Grandma!

Iboja blew the bedridden old woman a kiss and smiled.

Love with the permanent revolutionary was like groundwater. Giorgio appeared in their town a few times; once, when the bank granted Iboja permission to change money, he even took her to Milan by car. Giorgio tried to become a force on the battlefield of ideas about how to achieve a free world for everyone through stubborn resistance and private rebellion. But gradually people lost interest in him.

Humane and humanistic ideas became old-fashioned; the world of the powerful wanted everything to move more quickly—money especially, together with the desire to again change the boundaries of the world. Nostalgia for the old days of empire was supplanting the new ideals.

He lost his old enthusiasm.

Or perhaps he ended up with a white shirt, a short back and sides, a yappy Italian wife and jolly children in one of Milan's less exclusive quarters. After years of silence between them, Iboja realized that the bubbling water of hot feeling had remained submerged forever in the depths of great passion and dreams.

Meanwhile/fragment/between times

THE FLOWERY GIPSY'S DEADLY PARROT.

Sára and Mama.

After her husband's death of a heart attack, which came soon after her son-in-law died, Sára's grandmother started to talk to the little girl about the Creator. With an exalted, almost possessed voice, she told her grandaughter how necessary and helpful it was to talk to Him.

But why doesn't he speak to me first? And what does he want me to say? wondered the little girl.

He speaks to you mutely, in his own tongue! He is not silent, he's just waiting.

If I'm supposed to speak to God, I want to hear his voice! Like yours and Grandad's before he died. Otherwise I won't speak to him—I won't!

And the six-year-old beat her quilt with her fists and burst into tears because she felt something scratching her inside.

A few years later, when her grandmother was being buried, Sára stood by her grave mortified. She thought that God, reticent and unknown, was now punishing her for not wanting to talk to him.

Time passed in a grey and leaden fashion but Sára grew quickly. Days and years slipped by monotonously.

Sára later remembered how she hadn't really wanted to go to those noisy end-of-war celebrations where important men gave speeches, wreaths and bouquets were placed by the memorial on the square, a brass band played and people sang heroes' marching songs. Afterwards, the crowds of people bought frankfurters with mustard on paper trays, beer with shots of spirits and lemonade and candy floss for their children. Sára stood on the pavement with her mother, and people carrying little state flags and other paper-tasselled banners occasionally bumped into them or quietly dropped their flags on the ground. Sára did not want anything, though her mother drank some yellow lemonade from a waxed paper cup. And then an old gipsy woman in a blue floral skirt and bold red blouse with smaller flowers on it was suddenly walking straight towards them. She had a headscarf with a bright rosehip pattern tied tightly around her temples and her gold earrings were swinging from side to side. She smiled so widely at Sára's mother, the girl could see her rotten black teeth as well as two metal ones at the front. It was as if she had been looking for her for a long time.

So there you are, my beauty!

The gipsy opened her arms wide and the parrot on her shoulder screeched:

Bea-u-u-uty! The gipsy woman touched its beak and spoke as if she had known Sára's mother all her life:

You no longer have to struggle every day with fate. My little bird will choose one for you. And you must fulfil it—that is your true destiny.

And she lifted up a box with folded up scraps of paper inside and the parrot immediately passed one to Sára's mother with its beak. The gipsy then took the woman's hand and traced the long nail of her index finger along her palm lines.

My lovely little thing, he is never wrong! He has found your destiny for you. But I'll need a few hallers to feed the poor creature.

When she got what she wanted, she stuck her green-coated tongue out at Sára and disappeared into the crowd. The girl shuddered in terror.

Throw it away! It'll make you ill! she ordered her mother.

Sára, this is not something that you throw away.

And Emilka started laughing. But when she read the message, she furrowed her brow, rolled the paper into a ball and put it in her pocket. When Sára asked her what it said, her mother quickly changed the subject:

Let's buy a canary—let's buy two, in fact. They will sing to us in the kitchen, in the evening we will throw a scarf over them and during the day we will chirrup like they do—like I used to as a girl when I would go deep into the woods to imitate the birds. Perhaps you should study ornithology. It is one of the few beautiful occupations left in this wretched world.

Emilka was now prepared to irrevocably close the expanding empty space Imro had left behind—she could not go on any longer. At 4 a.m. she kissed her daughter like a moth so as not to wake her and pushed her hair away from her face. Leaving no note, she then quietly locked the door behind her and went towards the river. She was outside the town walking through a little park when she saw, scratched into the trunk of a birch tree, the initials of two names joined together with the + symbol and encircled by a heart. She saw it as a sign, ran her index finger over the rough inscription and staggered onwards. Halfway through her life she had lost her way. She was stuck in a dark forest and had lost all appetite for life. There was a cotton-wool cloud in her head reminding her of how, towards the end of Imro's life, she had stopped seeing his face when she looked into his eyes. Instead, she could only see his tortured soul and those feverish eyes of his burning through her—he was looking at her as if through that cotton-wool cloud, towards something opening up beyond her.

A strange vision of a large fluffy cloud with the head of an old man stretching across the cobalt space now came to her. It was like a floating deity of unknown strength and meaning. Perhaps it was Emilka's sublimated melancholy carved out of her head.

Sára would have probably forgotten all about the meeting with the fortune-teller but her mother had disappeared completely. She didn't come back after a week nor even after two. In fact, she didn't come back at all.

Sára recalled the ball of paper hidden in her mother's dress since the end-of-war anniversary celebrations in May when they had met that crazy gipsy woman and her parrot. But she could find nothing in the pockets of the dress hanging up in the wardrobe. She buried her face in its fabric, breathing in the scent of her mother's skin. And then she put the blue silon dress on and burst into tears.

A week, a fortnight and then a month passed without her mother returning . . . The unfamiliar faces Sára now saw every day were like masks and made her feel feverish with their questioning, searching for Mama, telephone calls . . . Now, as a teenager, she again recalled her stubborn refusal to talk to God. Before dawn, a snake of fear came slithering up to her together with voices of guilt and confusion. Perhaps it was these demons and the pains behind her breastbone which caused her to black out and then faint at her desk in class one day in autumn.

After losing consciousness, Sára woke up in hospital. Only once did she cry there—she was washing her face, remembered her mother and suddenly felt a hot jet on her mouth and chin. In the mirror she saw her bloodied lips and burst into tears. Her blood mixed with her tears, water, mucus and saliva.

Afterwards, difficult legal proceedings began in order to decide what to be done with the orphaned girl. During the process, Sára stayed with Iboja and her grandmother. In the end, Iboja lost in her struggle to have custody of the girl and Sára was sent to a children's home.

The home was in a Baroque manor house in the middle of what had once been a beautiful forest park but which no one now took care of. It had turned wild, like some of the girls sent there as if to a house of correction. Behind its thick walls, in spaces where damp and mould gathered, there hung permanent smells of soup, laundry and cleaning fluids.

Sára was put in a room with five other girls. She couldn't tell them apart but could feel their warmth when they secretly huddled up at night like abandoned animals even though the carers had forbidden it. They put their arms around each other's shoulders—the touch and smell of another person replaced something—someone they had lost and gave them a sense of peace and safety. If the carers came into the room at night, they would quickly separate them but because Sára was so good at school, they would turn a blind eye to it if she herself didn't mind sharing a bed. Later on though, as she grew, she could only sleep properly if she had a bed to herself.

On the higher floors were older girls of sixteen and seventeen. Sometimes in summer, especially during Midsummer night when all the beacons on the hills had burnt out, old women were out gathering herbs and young couples slipped into the nearby wood, a few boys still smelling of the fire they had been jumping over would climb the walls surrounding the park. The night was young, so they would run down from the hills to the manor, scramble through the bushes between the trees, hoot like night owls and climb up drainpipes and lightning conductors to the open windows of the rooms where their nocturnal lovers giggled as they waited. In their metal bedside lockers, they would hide pictures of naked men with their genitals highlighted, occasionally kissing them with histrionic sighs. But they expected no golden ferns from their nocturnal visitors. Sára didn't see it—she was never put in the same room as the 'wild things' (as they were called) but other girls told her about it, their cheeks burning with excitement and biting their nails as they spoke.

Sára very quickly found out that the nicest place in the manor was the library. It was in a room with strangely partitioned walls and an arch in the middle—this was what remained of the chapel belonging to the former owners of the manor who had religious services separate from the rest of the villagers. One of the carers worked as librarian if, in the afternoon, after finishing their duties, any of the girls wanted to come and read. She sat by the writing table, yawned with boredom or dozed off—she reminded Sára of an owl. If during the weekends it was pouring outside or there was a blizzard, the girls would come here more often to play Mikado or snap while the older ones would play draughts or rummy.

Sára had her own place in the armchair by the French window where it was always light for a long time and where she would sit tailor-fashion and read. When she stopped for a moment, she would look out at the overgrown bushes and exotic trees which no gardener had tended to for a long time and see changeable forms. Sometimes the carer left Sára all on her own, going out onto the terrace to drink coffee or have a cigarette with her colleagues. In the room was another high twin door which no one ever opened.

It rained that day, with drops rustling in the green outside the window and tapping on the glass. Sára stood up, walked to the mysterious door and grasped the handle. To her surprise it wasn't locked. Only there was no room behind it just an alcove with a semicircular wall about two metres in diameter. And like the thick, panelled jambs of the door, it was covered in paintings. Sára had the feeling that she had fallen into the magical colourful world of some tale which would never bore her and that she could keep coming back to as if to a small island that was all her own. The cramped space never seemed like a cell to her, a place where fugitives from monasteries would be put in solitary confinement after being caught or coming back voluntarily. She had read about something similar in an old book. She got hold of a torch so that when she next slipped unseen into her magical world, she could close the door behind her and stretch out on a blanket she had also brought.

At the base of one of the side panels was a lake or part of a bay with a craggy mountain range beyond it either covered in snow or completely iced over. And above it was a deep blue sky. Sára took off her socks, placed the soles of her feet on the stretch of water and imagined the waves lapping around her ankles. Perhaps people like her mother and father disappeared beyond those craggy white mountains after they died. She was rather sorry that she had never talked to anyone about death and what new worlds lay beyond it.

Did everyone have their own little island where they could listen to the heaving of the sea as if to music?

Above her head floated something that looked like the head of God in the religious pictures her grandmother had shown her. But attached to the head was a body that looked like an elongated conical shell or lantern of the same colour as the pointed mountains. It occurred to Sára that it was another god, a god of pagan people or sea creatures. And it was also lazily levitating in the same blue colour as that above the mountains. Sára liked turning onto her bottom the most, her knees pressed to her chin, and looking at the panels on the other side. In the infinity of the cobalt blue, there stood a gravity-free figure—neither male nor female, dressed like a page in slender burgundy velvet trousers, a white shirt and golden cape and with thick shoulder-length curls of hair of the same golden colour. Its face was sweet and similar to that of the angel who came to tell Mary she would give birth to a child and who Sára had seen on the cards her grandmother used to bookmark prayers. In one hand, the figure held a bow and in the other, an arrow aimed at some bull-like animal—as if he wanted to hit it in the eye. But the aggressive gesture was forever restrained like all the movements of everyone and everything in the pictures. Time here went at another pace and it was that which gave Sára most peace.

One day the old stoker saw Sára quietly squeezing the door handle while he was checking the radiators in the library. And he told her how, at one time, there were paintings on all the chapel walls like those in her secret alcove. Only after the war, when the manor was seized by the state with the last owners long out of the country, the orphanage was established and all the walls were painted white for hygienic reasons. After that, Sára did not stop going to her island where time passed quietly but she did start to imagine that she would return here one day and strip the walls of their layers of white paint. And beneath would reappear the colourful eyes of angels, saints and perhaps even God himself. She would see their clothes, their gestures and how they were all levitating in the blue sky. And at the very top of the dome there would perhaps be stars or floating clouds with cherubs sitting on them.

When Sára was eighteen, she was able to stay with Iboja, her grandmother and Auntie Zuzka during her last few months at secondary school.

After her *maturita* exam, she studied chemistry at university with a passion. From the very start, one rather clumsy boy there attracted her for the sole reason that he was even better at chemistry than she. Although she could sometimes barely follow his thought processes, the equations and formulae which he effortlessly came up with made absolute sense to her and aroused her interest.

They got married before they graduated, and, driven by ambition, fled to Italy just as Iboja's parents had once fled to France. They bought a holiday at a travel agency and did not come home. After a year, they managed to get to Germany.

Determination and a wolfish voracity, as Sára described it, enabled them to achieve success in Germany, specifically in the laboratory of the academic chemical institute where they worked. In their new home, the locals described them as 'come from the East' which reminded Sára of the tale of the Three Wise Men, though one had apparently left them in Italy. A few years later, they had a baby girl. Then, after long years of marriage, they got divorced. Sára still did not know how to talk out loud to the God of her grandmother and her old feelings of guilt for the death of her closest relatives and the loss of her husband came back to haunt her.

Archery was her only way of slowing down the workings of her mind which, in difficult situations, had the tendency to go faster than she could bear. Shooting an arrow outdoors somewhere, her mind became as focused and sharp as the tip of a pencil—and it was this that brought her the release of self-forgetting. It was rather like when she shut herself up in the painted alcove of the manor library. There the painted archer aiming at the bull's eye was her faithful companion.

Now/fragment/

IMAGE BURDEN.

The unknown woman 2.

During their last night together, Iboja and Sára drank rather a lot and Iboja could feel her head swimming though she had not had vertigo for a long time. So despite Sára's persuasions, she insisted on sleeping in her own flat. Sára walked her back through the slumbering town. On the main street, they met only a stray dog which trotted alongside them for a while as if waiting for something and a police patrol. The young policeman asked them if everything was all right and if anything had happened to them. Iboja replied with an icy laugh:

Oh you handsome young man! Has anything happened? The whole of life has happened to us, that's what! Life with all its terrible cargo if you must know! And it has all passed in a flash.

Iboja jabbed the air with her index finger then told Sára to go back because they were almost at the bottom of town. The policemen, bemused by her strange words, gallantly offered to accompany the other younger woman home. They were going that way—they had night duty at the station.

In the morning, Iboja woke up later than usual. The sun was breaking through the slats of the blinds into the bedroom and living room. She opened the window and looked down at the street where life was bubbling with its slow summer tempo. Most people were either at work or away on holiday. When she leaned out of the window, she could see that the stall selling tobacco and newspapers was still open. She quickly got dressed, put loose tea and boiling water into the teapot, took butter and jam from the fridge, sliced some bread and dashed out to buy cigarettes. She would have her breakfast later. She had long been in the habit of having her first cigarette before breakfast on the balcony overlooking the courtyard.

At the newsstand, the headline on the local newspaper caught her eye:

'Remains Found of a Woman Dead for Decades'.

She slipped the newspaper under her arm, paid for everything and hurried home barely noticing the fresh diamond air, the flies buzzing around her thinning red-dyed hair and the chirping of the sparrows.

She swept her breakfast things to the edge of the table so that she could open out the newspaper.

'Plumbers repairing a burst water pipe in the area between the former Hotel Aurora and synagogue yesterday came across the remains of a dead body lying about two metres under ground. According to the coroner, they are the remains of a woman aged between twenty-five and thirty who probably died a violent death about sixty years ago. Shreds of the Persian carpet in which the dead body was apparently wrapped have also been recovered.'

The space in Iboja's head painfully contracted as she read the article a second time. It did not take long, the air cooled and she was again standing in her grandparents' bedroom, a little girl unsettled by events of the evening, intuitively feeling that something like a steamroller was flattening all their lives and wondering, like Sára, if she would one day hear the voice of the one whose name cannot be uttered and be able to have a conversation with him. She recollected the two men in hats and coats going out through the side entrance into the hotel garden and carrying something like a long sack and she recognized the carpet, similar to the one the servant girl always used to beat before holidays in the inner courtyard of the hotel but never in the garden. She recalled that image in the winter garden and now it was suddenly a burden to her. She reached for her mobile to phone Sára but remembered that she had a meeting with her lawyer that morning to arrange the sale of the villa to the town. The town would then restore the building and open a museum there dedicated to her father. On the first floor it would devote some rooms to a display commemorating the holocaust, an event which had affected the vast majority of the town's Jewish inhabitants. The two women had agreed all this the previous day with the mayor of the town and other officials.

It occurred to her that she should go to the police to describe her childhood memory to them. But who would be interested in what a five-year-old girl had seen from the window of her grandparents' bedroom sixty-five years ago? And perhaps it would only make things worse for her grandfather! What if the police wanted to incriminate him in it as owner of the hotel close to which the body had been found?! Her grandfather had been forced to endure so much! Only she, Iboja, could now save him from further blame, just as it was she, years before, who would not let their blame for him jumping under the lorry be forgotten. Iboja had wanted the investigation to be reopened and her grandfather exonerated. But what now with those remains, with a woman's bones turning to dust, found near to the pipes of the water mains? All there was was her memory!

No!

Iboja banged her fist on the table.

No! I can't take it on! No, no, no!

And she kept banging her fist.

Jazz was coming from the kitchen radio—it was the only channel she listened to. And misgivings, like a worm, reentered her mind that had learnt to be open and direct. Who was the dead woman? Had no one missed her during all those years, no one come looking for her? How and why and in what circumstances did she die during the Festival of Lights before the Christmas of 1950? And given her remains were found so near to it, could she not have been staying in the hotel? Such a crime could not be ignored or swept beneath the shreds of Persian carpet; the remains could not be buried again and the bones hidden. What actually happened to the bones of unknown people found by accident? And it occurred to her that it really was something important. Those men wore the suits of the secret police and had been carrying a rolled-up carpet.

There should still be records of those appalling policemen! And facts about them which were never meant to be uncovered!

It occurred to Iboja that someone wanted her to solve this problem. But who!? The whole of life is a jigsaw puzzle of fragments, sharp pieces, details, so many of which only make sense—if they make any sense, when they are all put together! But it also works the other way round—from one perfectly observed detail, you may sometimes deduce everything!

Iboja smoked hard, drank her cold tea but had no appetite for food. She changed into a smarter dress and went to the bathroom to put on some grey eye shadow and lipstick, powder her ashen face and brush her wiry, unmanageable hair. She had to sort out this business, on behalf of the unknown young woman and those unknown people who somewhere must have missed her. Why was it her as a five-year-old who had been fated to witness that nocturnal scene? It had happened before she even knew what time was. But the memory had come back with redoubled force, like an indelible image. And the image was a burden to her, a heavy load. But before she went out, she did what she always did when she felt the onset of chaos: she got out her accordion, closed the windows and drew the curtains. Everything became indistinct in the half-light. The world outside faded and time stood still.

She started to play. First she tapped out the simple melody: '*Limbora, Limbora*, your nuts are falling over our garden wall'. Then she opened out the accordion, so that it whined with pain, and ran her fingers wildly over the bass notes on the left before again squeezing it shut. She let it growl, wheeze heavily then roar like a rabid animal, flow like water, cry like a newborn, laugh and cheer. These were the abstract, unmelodic sounds of human feelings pulled tight, like a red thread, since the Stone Age.

Now/fragment/

BULL'S EYE.

Departure.

The alarm went off at half-past four. Sára got up immediately, wanting to be out with her bow before five in her belief that the world was at its most peaceful then. The reflex bow was already strung—she always carried it with her on her travels. She had left her longbow at home, which she used more often for training. This one had a wooden grip and thinner string easier to draw.

She washed herself with soap and cold water to the waist and rubbed her skin pink with a little frotte handtowel. She looked at the mirror on the wall.

I see an autumnal crow, she growled sardonically.

She was convinced she had something crow-like about her, whether it was the darkness of her skin, her sharp nose or the delicate sadness a flock of crows in autumn is shrouded in. Almost every morning, she realized without self-pity why her husband had left her for a younger, prettier woman. Perhaps she let him rub his sperm into her beautiful long thick hair. A long time ago he had done it to her once, but she had got her hair cut the next day.

When she had told Iboja the night before about her husband leaving her for another woman, Iboja fumed:

He had a charming, clever wife, the idiot! But she'll give him a hard time, don't you worry! Second marriages often finish even worse than first ones. But it's too late now to help the old fool!

Or he'll give her a hard time. Second wives usually have to put up with more.

Sára surprised Iboja with her contrariness.

Oh great! You're going to stand up for her are you—the woman who took your husband from you and wouldn't let him go?

It's not always like that, Iboja. It's not always the woman's doing!

Sára suddenly started to wonder how many more years of life her ex-husband had and what destiny awaited him. What if he got that same long and sad illness which Iboja's mother suffered from? Although it was Iboja who was really suffering, of course—her mother knew nothing. She had even lost all sensitivity to physical pain.

He would forget where he had left things. He would put his dentures in the fridge, a yogurt on the bookshelf. In the laboratory, she would notice his baffled, uncertain face through the glass of test tubes and see how he was losing his sharp intelligence, how his eyes were losing their spark and becoming empty. His face would become as blank as a dead fish and he would be constantly losing his keys; and he would stop answering people's questions or if he did, his answers would be vague and slow. He would withdraw into himself, be unable to find his way home and no longer recognize his wife. Later, as paranoia set in, he would be violent towards her, suspect her of having lovers and chase her out of the flat. He would forget his name and stare blankly into the middle distance at something no one else could see. Some hands would change his nappies, wash and dress him, hand him his tablets, food and tea. Towards the end, he would forget to eat and then even to swallow and he would get a catheter . . . Her imagination was so vivid she started to cry in her pity for him.

To hell with it! If that was to happen to me, I'd go completely mad! Iboja is right.

She almost hissed at the mirror as she angrily brushed her hair.

Yesterday, she let slip to Iboja how she had seen him with his beautiful young wife shopping for a handbag. She couldn't decide between two so he, the scatterbrained scientist who had gone to his lab his whole working life with just the same shabby old briefcase, bought her both. Iboja, feisty old Iboja with her great sense of justice, got even angrier when she heard:

You should have beaten them both on the heads with those handbags. I would have! she shouted, pouring cognac down her throat.

Today they would meet before her journey. Iboja would take Sára to the station, they would share a bittersweet embrace and Iboja would say to Sára as usual:

I hope that next year we will both still be above ground!

And she would soften her words with a laugh. Sára would then board the train and the two sisters would wave to each other. And the train would soon leave the station and the whole town fade into the distance as Iboja stood on the fast-emptying platform which had been witness to so many events, sounds and voices.

With the bow under her arm, Sára walked barefoot across the grass, a quiver with sixteen arrows hanging diagonally around her waist. Mixed with the scent of the grass, the dew was fragrant and cool underfoot. Sára could somehow smell everything: dew, air, the morning light, plants and most of all, the trees. She fastened the colourful paper target to the bargeboard of the summerhouse, went back about thirty metres and then started what was like a dance ritual with exactly the same movements and rhythm: taking out the arrow, pressing it to the string, pulling it back and then releasing the three fingers that held it. The arrow flew out but she stood motionless, watching it until its metal point penetrated the target. And then the other arrows followed, one by one, until they were all clustered together in the black inner circle of the target. That moment when she forgot about herself, the target and the arrow, when her movement and breathing came together with absolute precision, was her favourite of all. A Zen monk had once told her:

In Zen archery, the bowman and the target are not two objects in opposition but are one and the same. The bowman ceases to be aware of himself as someone intent on striking the bull's-eye controlling him. That state of unconsciousness can only be achieved when the person is completely freed from himself and his overloaded mind.

She went back inside as the dark-blue, orangey light was starting to turn white. She again felt strong and peaceful as she always did after the experience of coming closer to that kind of secret which cannot be cracked open like a nut with a hammer. It was a completely different secret from the ones people now enjoyed voraciously watching all kinds of horror and suspense on the plasma rectangles in their living room and feeling special because they had guessed the secret of the shallow plot before the film ended.

She would make some coffee and again drink it in the garden. The sun would be higher in the sky and there would be more light and birdsong. She would nibble a biscuit with her coffee and lower her eyelids. She would commune with her people, those who in that place were closer to her than anywhere else in the world.

She would sit in the paradise of this overgrown garden with her mother; her father would be standing to one side and then all the others—they would be there and at the same time they wouldn't and that was beautiful! All of those who were outside her because she did not know them, or had known them for only a short time, had remained within her—in her genes, in her memories, in that important place of not forgetting and of transmitting all that was past. They would speak a wordless language together.

Rather like the way the ancient Chinese used to drink hot water—tea without tea.

Sára smiled at the analogy which had come to her mind. She believed implicitly that her forbears had given her her free thinking, her determination in the workplace and her feeling for the lightness and playfulness of life. She had come here, to her parents' and grandparents' house and would keep returning here, to her father's pictures and everything else of his she was guardian of. The legacy of her forbears would help transform future generations' under-standing of the vicissitude and meandering course of human exis-tence. She tried to convince herself of it.

Without quite knowing why, she suddenly thought back to a lit-up garden on the large terrace of a seaside hotel where couples were dancing to Balkan music, some of whom were kissing, some drinking beer and cocktails, others singing or just sitting. They were looking out at the darkening sea and peach-coloured sky—as she had done with her ex-husband years before.

But Sára felt neither sadness nor anger at the image. Instead she breathed in, put her hands to her mouth and loudly, benevo-lently called out to someone, to something in the huge space sur-rounding her:

Hello! Hello!

Hell-o-o-o-o-o-o-o-o-o-o!